Gabriel stepped forward, and before Gillian could turn away, he had taken her face between his hands. His touch washed through her veins, flooding her senses with his strength and nearness.

"Your house...these treasures," Gillian murmured. "It's like nothing I've ever seen...."

His fingers slid through her hair. She could see the slow rise and fall of his chest where his robe parted, and the strong cords of his neck. His face was a mere breath away; his heat infused her. Her heart was pounding so hard, she was sure he could see her chest shake with the force of it.

"Who are you?" she whispered hoarsely.

His eyes were deep with passion; his thighs brushed hers.

"Your dream come true," he said softly.

Dear Reader,

You're about to meet one of the most mysterious, magical men!

Gabriel is many things, but none of them is ordinary, as Gillian Aldaire—and you—are about to find out.

And neither is any of the four heroes in American Romance's new MORE THAN MEN series. Whether their extraordinary powers enable them to grant you three wishes, communicate with dolphins or live forever, their greatest power is that of seduction.

So turn the page—and be seduced by a romantic man named Gabriel.

It's an experience you'll never forget!

Regards,

Debra Matteucci
Senior Editor & Editorial Coordinator

# Rebecca Flanders
## FOREVER ALWAYS

# Harlequin Books

TORONTO • NEW YORK • LONDON
AMSTERDAM • PARIS • SYDNEY • HAMBURG
STOCKHOLM • ATHENS • TOKYO • MILAN
MADRID • WARSAW • BUDAPEST • AUCKLAND

ISBN 0-373-16517-X

FOREVER ALWAYS

This edition published by arrangement with Harlequin Enterprises B. V.

® and TM are trademarks of the publisher. Trademarks indicated with ® are registered in the United States Patent and Trademark Office, the Canadian Trade Marks Office and in other countries.

Printed in U.S.A.

# Chapter One

Gillian Aldair was not prepared to die. She realized this only moments after the earth around her feet began to give way and she tumbled, flailing and fighting, down an eight-hundred-foot slope from which there was very little chance of emerging alive.

Only a fool would venture into the Andes without expecting danger, and Gillian was not a fool. She had traversed some of the most hostile terrain in South America over the past two weeks and she was aware, as was everyone else on the archaeological team, of the risks she took. But she couldn't anticipate everything. No one could.

That was small consolation when she had reached for purchase on protruding stone to help herself up the steep path and had felt the earth beginning to crumble beneath her feet.

It all happened very fast. She cast a quick frantic glance over her shoulder at Saim, her guide, and saw his normally placid brown face split with terror as the rumble of loose boulders and shifting ground began to roar toward him. Gillian flailed for balance and lost; she felt herself tumbling backward. Dirt filled her mouth and nose and sharp stones battered her as the ground took on a life of its own and carried her on its relentless brutal current down the sharp incline. Dimly she heard Saim's scream, horribly cut off. She felt an explosive pain in her left shoulder as she bounced against the side of the cliff and was, for a sickening moment, airborne. She landed with her right leg twisted beneath her and felt it snap.

Helplessly she rolled over and over, stabbed and battered on every side, choking on dust and the taste of her own blood, and her last thought before blessed darkness overtook her was tinged with faint surprise, for she had never expected it to happen like this. Not like this.

THE PAIN DRAGGED HER back into consciousness on its relentless, red-black tide, forcing her into a grim, though surprisingly calm, assessment of her situation. It was the stillness that struck her first. The utter, absolute absence of sound, movement or life. Isolation. Aloneness.

She tried to call out for Saim, but only a gurgling sound escaped her lips. Broken ribs stabbed with every shallow breath, and the desperate pressure on her right side was from a collapsed lung. She had not been married to a physician for eight years without recognizing the symptoms of a critically injured patient, even when the patient was herself.

She was lying half-buried beneath the rubble of the slide, and she could not tell whether her inability to move—or even feel—her legs was due to the weight pressing down on them or to the seriousness of her injuries. But when she turned her head to look down the length of her body, she could see her jeaned leg protruding at an unnatural angle. The mere sight of it made her nauseated. The flaming core of agony in her right upper body spoke of a shattered shoulder, and that arm was drenched in blood.

She tried to move her right leg, to wiggle her toes, to even feel something below the waist. She could not. Her back was probably broken.

She had lost her backpack, and with it her emergency supplies and her canteen. Shock had lowered her body temperature and with nightfall would come an even deeper cold. With nightfall would come the predators whose cries she had learned to ignore from the safety of her tent. The cougars, the bears...

She was half a day away from the base camp. Her team would not even begin to search for her until tomorrow afternoon. By that time it would be far, far too late.

It was becoming harder and harder to breathe. The shadows around her seemed to lengthen, but in her semidelirious state she could not tell whether that was due to the passage of time or impending unconsciousness. And because she didn't know how much longer she could fight back the blackness that threatened with each new wave to drag her under, she made a desperate effort to focus her strength, dragging herself up onto one elbow. But her head had barely left the ground before she collapsed again in a paroxysm of cold sweat and spinning agony, helpless to fight the blackness that was dragging her down again.

That was when she knew without a doubt how very much she did not want to die.

SHE FADED IN AND OUT of delirium. In her nightmares the tigers came, and pain took the form of lapping flames that consumed her flesh. Her husband, Jerry, dead two years now, looked down on her from a distant mist, and his expression was disappointed.

"I'm sorry, Jerry," she mumbled. "I'm sorry...."

She reached for him, but he retreated from her, moving backward through the mist, the sadness in his eyes lingering long after his features had faded away. When the tigers came again, with their slavering jaws and gleaming red eyes she was almost glad.

The twilight was cold and purple, and pain was like a dozen dull-edged knives, sawing at various parts of her body. Each breath she took, the pulse of her heart sliced a little deeper, opened new raw nerve endings to the flames. The breath of the tigers that crouched over her was hot and she welcomed it. She couldn't fight any longer.

And then one of the tigers spoke, its tone soft with wonder and hinted with urgency. "She lives, Malik."

Said its companion, "Quickly then. Move back."

And while Gillian puzzled over this with a dim and distant interest, something remarkable happened. The face of the tiger that now bent over her began to change, to shift and melt into the features of a man. At the same time, a sensation spread through her that was like being engulfed in a golden wave, as though her blood were being replaced with liquid sunshine, and as the wave rose higher, as the liquid pulsed through her veins, the pain was engulfed, swallowed by warmth and blessed contentment. That was when she realized the face above hers was that of much more than just a man.

The features were sharp and cleanly defined, the cheekbones high, the forehead broad, the lips full. His skin was golden brown, a natural tan that might come from moderate exposure to the sun at this elevation. His neck was a strong sturdy column, his shoulders broad and bronzed. Gillian could see the movement of the strong tendons beneath his clavicle as he worked over her, clearing away the rubble that trapped her, touching her with hands she could not feel. His hair was honey brown streaked with gold, and it was long and thick, falling well below his shoulders, making a veil that sometimes shielded his face from her when he bent low. And she hungered to see his face again, to memorize it, to worship it. It was the face of a man who took away the pain, who gave her a chance to live again just when she had come to realize how very precious life was. It was the face of an angel.

"Who are you?" she tried to ask, but the words came out as nothing more than an unintelligible croak, a groan that was barely audible through lips that were swollen and caked with blood.

He turned to her. His hair swung away to reveal his face, and his expression was quiet and strong and oddly gentle. His eyes were azure blue, the color of a Mediterranean sea where no wind blows, calm and timeless and breathtakingly beautiful.

He said softly, "It's all right, little one. You are safe now."

She believed him. She drifted into sleep, dreaming of his eyes and the musical sound of his voice.

GILLIAN AWOKE in a softly lit room with the memory of gentle dreams floating around her like clouds. She was warm, she was comfortable, she was surrounded by softness, and at first she thought she must be in her parents' home in Virginia. The eiderdown comforter, the pale green wallpaper, the feather mattress... She could almost hear early morning birdsong through the open window, and smell the lilac that bloomed just outside. Her first instinct was to burrow deeper into the pillow, reveling in that pleasant borderland between wake and sleep until the smell of coffee summoned her downstairs.

But something kept nagging at her, forcing her into wakefulness. She realized first there was no window, no birdsong. When she opened her eyes and made them focus, she saw nothing but yellow gauze, and she blinked to clear her vision. Then she realized her bed was canopied with a profusion of romantic netting that was drawn back in places with gilded medallions, festooned and draped overhead so that the impression was indeed like floating on a cloud.

The bed itself was a massive four-poster adorned by gilded cherubs and an abundance of climbing vines on the posts and head- and footboards, all of it elaborately painted in gold and white in the manner of the baroque era. The wallpaper appeared to be silk and it, too, was a gold-and-white tapestry. Just like a fairy-tale palace, she thought drowsily.

She turned over in bed and that was when she remembered. The expedition. The landslide. The pain...

The man with the beautiful face.

Her shoulder had been shattered, her ribs and leg fractured. Those things she knew for certain. In all probability, her spine had also been broken. She shouldn't have been able to turn over at all. Yet there was no pain. No traction equipment, no IV drip, no cast...

What had happened to her? Where *was* she?

Cautiously, she sat up, expecting an explosion of pain in the arm she used to brace herself, in the back she carefully straightened, in the hip upon which she rested her weight. It never came. Her muscles were a little stiff, as though she had been sleeping for a long time, but other than that all she felt was hungry. Ravenous, in fact.

She pushed a lock of her heavy dark hair away from her face and grimaced at the stiff feel of it. She definitely needed a shampoo. She should have cut her hair before starting on the expedition, but Jerry had liked her hair long and she was sentimental.

The expedition. How in the world had she gotten from the barren terrain of the Andes to this ornate bedchamber? *Where* in the world was she?

*No,* she thought, looking again around the room with its frescoed ceiling and crystal lamps and Persian carpets, *I've got to be dreaming.* Just how much, exactly, of the last hours of her memory had she dreamed?

But she had not dreamed the expedition that had been ten months in the making. Crandon Stiles, David Marsh and Ellen Chadwell had approached her about joining their search for the mysterious Lost Tribe of the Andes shortly after Jerry's death. She should have been flattered to be included among such illustrious company, but the enthusiasm she managed was forced. She had agreed out of duty, not desire.

She had not imagined her mother's anxiety, or the concern that her father had disguised beneath gruff approval. Inactive in the field since shortly after college, she was going to one of the most isolated, dangerous regions of the world, and they were right to be worried.

She hadn't imagined the months of paperwork, the shots, the goodbyes, the flight into the wilderness, the selection of their native crew, the ascent into the mountains, the physical hardship, the slow acclimation. Heated discussions over freeze-dried dinners, maps and research papers spread out over a camp table and studied by the light of a lantern. The noises of the night creatures that stalked their camp as she tossed and turned alone in her tent. The isolation, the loneliness, the desperation to lose herself in her work. She hadn't imagined any of that.

But the man with the blue eyes?

She was wearing a plain white nightgown of some soft natural fiber that looked like muslin but was woven much finer. The sleeves were long and loose, and there was no decoration whatsoever. Given the ornate character of the room, Gillian was relieved to find her own attire so simple. At least she could be assured she was not dreaming all of this.

There was only one possible explanation. There had been an accident, though obviously not as serious as she had thought. Someone had found her and brought her here. But where was here? And Saim, her guide. Had he been rescued, too?

She was almost persuaded to try out her legs—one of which she had once been convinced was broken in at least two places—and go in search of answers, when there was a click, and she turned her head in time to see the gold-paneled door open. A dark-skinned young woman entered, bearing a round wooden tray laden with food. Her eyes flew wide with surprise and uncertainty when she saw Gillian sitting up.

"Hello," Gillian said.

Her attention was equally divided between the tray and the woman who brought it, for although scientific curiosity was a compulsion, hunger was even more demanding. The native girl was short, with the soft, round figure and gleaming, healthy dark hair that characterize a diet high in fat and a life-style that does not depend upon hunting for survival. She wore a loose, floor-length garment like a muumuu, dyed a brilliant shade of turquoise and ornamented with bright yellow embroidery. Her features were square and squat, faintly reminiscent of Mayan characteristics, her eyes large, dark and almond-shaped. The woman did not resemble any of the native tribes Gillian had encountered thus far in her explorations, and she would not have expected to find someone of her body type at this elevation.

But the succulent aromas emanating from the tray made it all but impossible to concentrate on anything but the empty pit that was her stomach. There was a bowl piled high with fruit in the center of the tray, and a woven basket next to it held a dark, moist bread that was still steaming from the oven. A round of cheese was covered by a glass dome, and a soup tureen accompanied it. The scent was so inviting, the longing made her weak, and it was all Gillian could do to keep herself from snatching the tray from the girl.

Instead she said, "It smells wonderful. Have you been taking care of me? I want to thank you."

The girl gave her a timid, hesitant smile as she placed the tray on the ornate marble-topped table beside Gillian's bed. It occurred to Gillian that the girl might not speak English. And why should she? This was, the last time she had checked, Peru.

Yet knowing that, Gillian was still compelled to chatter, mostly to keep the pangs of hunger at bay. "I don't suppose you could tell me where I am. Or who found me. Or how long it's been since I've eaten. I'm starving."

The girl poured what appeared to be red wine into a carved bronze cup and offered it to Gillian. When Gillian took it with murmured thanks, the girl indicated the food on the tray with an awkward gesture of her hand, then hurriedly backed away. She ran the last few steps out the door.

Gillian's curiosity over the girl's behavior did not last long, for the demands of her hunger were by far more pressing. She tasted the contents of the cup and found it to be more of a nectar than a wine. Its delicious sweetness was surprisingly energizing; she could feel strength and well-being flowing into her muscles almost as soon as she swallowed. She tore off a chunk of the bread and spread it thickly with the cheese, forcing herself to eat slowly. It was, without a doubt, the most delicious thing she had ever tasted.

She was halfway through the soup when the door opened again. By this time her hunger was sufficiently satisfied that she could take more detailed notice of her visitor. Like the woman who had come before him, he wore a long shapeless robe, though his was white. Though his nut-brown skin proclaimed him to be a native, nothing else about his features suggested he might be of the same tribe as the girl. His head was bald, his eyes brown, his smile broad. His small nose and well-defined lips almost suggested a European background. And though the full cut of his robe did not entirely conceal a certain plumpness, his figure had the appearance of having been obtained through a love of fine dining rather than genetics. Gillian's anthropologist's mind took all of this in at a glance and filed it away for future reference, for there were of course more important matters on her mind than this man's ethnic origins.

She swallowed quickly and put down her spoon. "Hello," she said. "Is this your house? Where am I?"

"Ah," replied the man in an accent that was lyrically intonated, "you are English. It is good. A chance to practice."

"I'm American, actually," she replied cautiously. "My name is Gillian Aldair."

He bowed from the waist. "Our pleasure to serve, Mademoiselle Gillian. Have you all you need?

"I'd love a cup of coffee."

A small frown touched his smooth brow. "Coffee?"

"Never mind. Really, everything is perfect." She made a gesture toward her surroundings that was meant to convey awe. "The room, the food...it's wonderful. But how did I get here? The last thing I remember, there was a landslide.... Was there an airlift out?"

He looked slightly puzzled at the word *airlift,* but responded. "You were injured. We found you and brought you here."

"And Saim? Is he all right?"

A look of sadness crossed the man's face, and she knew the answer before he spoke. "If you refer to your companion, we were too late to save him."

Gillian's throat tightened as she thought of the native who had so cheerfully volunteered to accompany her on her journey up the mountainside. He wouldn't be going home again. Except for the grace of God and this man, she presumed neither would she.

Gillian looked at him again, more carefully this time, studying him. "You're the one who found me?"

He inclined his head.

"But there is someone else."

His pleasant, round face revealed nothing.

"A man . . . with long brown hair and blue eyes." She spoke carefully, searching the man's face for a reaction. She was aware of a tightening in her chest, a slight speeding of her heart, as though dreading his denial—or his confirmation.

He said gently. "You have been very ill, missy. You will eat and rest."

Gillian frowned faintly with remembrance, bringing back the details with surprising ease. His face. How could she forget his face? "He gave me something—morphine maybe—and the pain went away."

Still he only smiled. "I know not this morphine."

"I remember thinking he was an angel," Gillian murmured.

"There is a bathing chamber adjoining this one," her companion said. "When you have finished with your supper, I will send a girl to assist you." He turned as though to go.

"Wait," Gillian said. She couldn't let him leave her like this, with more questions unanswered now than when he had entered. "What's your name?"

Again he made her a polite little bow. "I am called Phillipe."

Was it a trace of French she heard in his accent? "Is this your house?" she asked.

He smiled. "Ah, yes, here I live. We all do."

"No, I mean, do you own it?" He looked puzzled and she clarified, "Did you build it?"

The puzzlement cleared into a kind of ingenuous understanding. "Ah, you mean it is the house of Malik."

Malik. She had heard that name before. "Is he the man who found me?" she persisted. "The one with the hair—the blue eyes?"

"You rest now, *mademoiselle.*"

"Will you take me to see him? I need to talk to him—to thank him for all he's done, and—"

But Phillipe's face had gone blank, like a door closing off the light of a room. "Malik will not be disturbed."

"What do you mean he won't be disturbed? He brings an injured stranger into his house—saves her life—and then he can't be bothered to say hello? I think you'd better check with him on that one!"

"There is no need. It is not necessary for you to talk to him."

She stared at him. "Well, I damned sure need to talk to somebody! And since you don't seem to have any answers—"

"You will tire yourself." He turned to go, then stopped to straighten a painting in a gilded frame that hung on the wall adjacent to her bed.

"Lovely, isn't it?" He smiled, stepping back to admire the art. "It is one of my favorites. It is by a man named Vincent van Gogh, who Malik says is a very fine artist, and very famous. Malik has many of his paintings."

Gillian stared at Phillipe. She stared at the painting. "He has *many* van Goghs?"

Phillipe smiled at her. "I shall go now. Don't weary yourself."

"No, please—don't go! How long have I been here? Where is this place?"

She pushed aside the covers and started to slide out of bed. As she did so, her nightgown rode up above her knees and she stopped, staring at her leg.

Just below her right knee on the shin was a round, jagged-edge scar, and a fainter narrow scar several inches long below it—the kind of scar that might be produced by a compound fracture of the tibia and the resultant surgical repair. The kind of fracture Gillian had imagined she had seen in her own right leg after the landslide.

But it would have taken months for the scar to reach this stage of healing. She had not had the scar before she came to this place.

She looked up at Phillipe slowly. "How long have I been here?" she repeated hoarsely.

"A short time," he assured her cheerfully. He came forward and began to rearrange the sheets, gently urging her back against the pillows.

"How long?" she demanded, a little wildly now.

"Days," he insisted soothingly. "A mere handful of days."

"That's impossible." But now her voice was barely a whisper as she stared at him.

"Your strength will return," he promised her. "Now you rest."

"No," she said. "I want some answers."

But her voice had lost its authority; tinged with uncertainty, it sounded more querulous than demanding, and it obviously did not impress him.

He smiled as he moved toward the door. "I will send a girl," he said. "They do not speak English as nice as me, but they will understand your wishes."

Gillian's hand crept beneath the covers, rubbing the scar on her leg. "Wait," she called out uncertainly. But by the time she did, the door was already closing behind him.

She closed her eyes against the spinning images that whirled through her head. Piercing blue eyes. A stopped clock. Vincent van Gogh. Tumbling rocks, the memory of pain, a strong, handsome face... Questions, so many questions.

But the answers were here, somewhere in this house, with a man called Malik. And she intended to find them.

THE ROOM IN WHICH HE SAT was large and circular; its walls were of stone and its ceiling so high it disappeared into the shadows. Heavy tapestries adorned the walls and embroidered draperies divided the chamber into smaller spaces. The bed was carved from massive oak posts and draped with furs. There were candles flickering in sconces on the walls and strategically placed braziers burning around the room, although both heat and light were derived from other sources. Though many might have found the atmosphere created by the dark oversize furnishings and stone walls and floors a forbidding one, he liked the room because it reminded him of a time he had once been happy.

The security monitor was a startling anachronism in such a place, and he made use of it as seldom as possible. As soon as Phillipe left her room, he turned the monitor off and replaced the carved wooden panel that concealed it inside the wide oak desk. He turned away, looking at nothing in particular, his expression thoughtful.

She was an American. He had thought she might be, and that pleased him. She was also very curious, and that could be unfortunate.

Perhaps it would have been wiser not to rush quite so quickly to the site of the landslide. And having discovered the girl clinging to life by such a fragile thread, perhaps he should have turned away and let nature take its course. The wilderness was a hostile place. The creatures within it lived out their short, violent lives and met their brutal deaths every day and he had never intervened before. No doubt he would come to regret his weakness on this occasion. Indeed, so might she.

But he had seen her lying there, her poor body crushed and broken almost beyond repair, clinging so bravely, so foolishly to life when any sensible soul would have long since given up, and he was moved.

Few things in this world had the power to touch his inner heart these days, but she had done so and without even trying. Perhaps it would prove to be a mistake, bringing her here, but he was glad to know he could still make mistakes in the name of compassion. Humanity.

He heard the soft sound of Phillipe's footsteps on the stone floor and turned toward it. Phillipe pushed aside a drapery and came into the area where he sat.

"She concerns me, Malik," he said without preamble. He spoke in French, the language he was most comfortable with. "I think it would have been better to take her back to her friends while she slept. It is still not too late...."

The other man gestured toward the monitor, his expression placid. "Her friends have given up the search, broken camp. Who can blame them? The landslide blocked the trail and they don't have the equipment to cross it—even if they did have reason to believe she survived." He shrugged eloquently. "There is no one to return her to, my friend. Would you have me deposit her in the jungle and leave her to the monkeys and cats?"

Phillipe frowned uncomfortably. "I have never met one such as she."

The other man smiled, with a peculiar sort of gentleness that softened his angular features and bore not a trace of bitterness. "She called me an angel," he murmured. "I have been called many things in my lifetime, Phillipe, but never that."

But then his focus returned to the present, and the familiar cynical twist settled itself on his lips once again. "If only she knew, eh, old friend?"

"What is to be done with her, Malik?" Phillipe asked soberly. "She is no longer a broken bird to be coaxed back into life. She is strong enough to beat her wings against her cage and clever enough to refuse captivity. And this bird, I think, could tear our eyes out if she took it into her mind to do so."

A soft chuckle was his reply. "I think you may be right."

Phillipe shifted his weight from one foot to the other, looking uncomfortable. It had been a long time since he had heard the other man laugh, and that only increased his uneasiness. His small hands were clasped tightly together as he searched for the right words. "She concerns me, Malik. She is..." And here self-expression seemed to fail him. "She is like you."

A swift, sharp frown marred the other man's features, and he replied harshly, "No one is like me."

But after a moment his brow cleared, and his troubled expression faded into thoughtfulness that was faintly imbued with pleasant remembrance as he added, "But she is interesting, is she not? One might even say... fascinating."

"She asks many questions," Phillipe insisted stubbornly. "I don't know what to tell her."

The one he called Malik regarded him with friendly amusement for a moment, pretending to consider this. "Tell her the truth," he replied after a time.

Phillipe repeated carefully, "The truth."

"About everything but me, of course," he qualified. "Try to avoid that subject if you can."

Phillipe's expression was dubious. "That may prove difficult."

"What is life without challenge?"

"You are quite certain."

"The lady is our guest. She will be treated as such—with certain restrictions, of course."

"And you would have me answer her questions."

And once again he smiled, encouragingly. "You worry too much, Phillipe. What harm can it do to enjoy the company of such a lovely, spirited young woman for a time? Practice your English, let her regale you with tales of things you will never see, bring the women and children to marvel at her.... Such diversions are far too rare in our little corner of the world, are they not?"

This time Phillipe frowned, his disapproval evident. "You make light of what can be very serious. She is here, she will ask questions, she will learn of us..."

"And what point is there in trying to deceive her? You are a lamentable liar, Phillipe, and she is too clever to be fooled for long. Besides, if there is one thing I have learned about human beings, it is that truth is almost always the last thing they will believe."

But the smile faded slightly and became tinged with something almost like sorrow. His eyes once again seemed to be looking toward something far away as he added softly, "I suspect Miss Gillian Aldair is no exception."

## Chapter Two

Gillian waited until late in the evening. She waited until the artificial lighting, of its own accord, dimmed and disappeared and left the room lit only by the painted china bedside lamps, and still she waited, straining for sounds of movement in the corridor outside her room. Her heart was beating hard, partly with excitement and partly with dread, as she forced herself to wait still longer.

Finally she swung her feet to the floor and moved to the door, opening it slightly. She listened for sounds of movement before venturing to peek beyond the door, but heard none. Cautiously she slipped outside.

She wasn't surprised to find the corridor outside her room was pitch-dark, and she wondered if she should go back for a lamp. But as her feet stepped across the threshold, the corridor lighting seemed to adjust itself, as though an electric eye had sensed her presence. Amazed, she stepped back into her room and darkness fell. She crossed into the corridor again and a gentle light came on. Yet it wasn't really a light at all—more like a moonlit night, with dark blue shadows etched in silver light. It was still and silent and strangely compelling.

She moved down the corridor, her bare feet whispering on the stone floor. Yet those whispers seemed to echo, announcing her presence to anyone who wanted to hear, and she found herself sticking close to the shadows, which was even more disorienting. *No one ordered me to stay in my room,* she told herself firmly, bolstering her courage. The doors weren't locked. She had every right to walk around if she wanted. And if someone found her, she would tell him… What? She was just going down to the fridge for a snack?

The bravado with which she had left her quarters began to edge away as she moved farther and farther from the comforting glow of lamplight. The artificial moonlight, while enchanting, had a surreal, otherworldly quality that was unnerving. Everything looked different in this light. And as she took one turn and then another, she began to wonder just how reliable her memory was, and what would become of her if she got lost.

And then she saw an archway, and tall wooden doors beneath. She did not know whether to feel relief or dread. She hesitated, glancing back over her shoulder, almost persuaded to call the whole thing off for tonight and try again tomorrow. But then she squared her shoulders and gathered her fortitude. She had never been a quitter; that was one of the things Jerry had most admired about her. And this was certainly no time to discover a heretofore unsuspected streak of cowardice.

Gillian moved into the arch and seized the cold iron handle of one of the doors. She suspected that it would be locked, and that would be that. But the door opened inward without even a squeak of a rusty hinge. Cautiously Gillian stepped through and found herself in another corridor.

It was wide and lined with smooth gray stones, unlike the outer one which had been of gleaming marble. Glass-globed sconces several feet above her head provided dim illumination, just enough to give her shadow eerie dimensions as she moved. There were other arched entrances on either side of her, but there was nothing but darkness beyond, and she ignored them. She moved toward the faint hint of warm light at the end of the hallway.

The light led her through another set of double arches and into a room hung ceiling-to-floor with heavy tapestries, Oriental rugs and filmy draperies. The rugs and draperies formed walls, she realized, rooms within a much larger room, a treatment that reminded her of the way an avant-garde decorator might design a New York loft. But this was not New York, and this definitely was not a yuppie's city loft.

There was the very faintest haze of smoke in the air, and as Gillian followed the pattern formed by cloth walls into another room area, she saw two braziers burning with warm yellow flames. The smoke was scented with something exotic and faintly familiar—sandalwood, she realized eventually. That had always seemed to her a very warm and masculine scent.

In sconces along the walls fat candles flickered, casting tall shadows on the woven carpets covering the floor and the portraits and objets d'art on the wall. The dark, heavy furniture combined to produce an overall effect that was medieval in tone, yet...somehow more. There was a silver service on a table beside a high-backed chair, and as she watched, the chair slowly began to turn, swiveling around to face her.

It was him.

Gillian smothered a small gasp, but she couldn't stop herself before taking a startled step back. She thought the room was unoccupied. And until that moment, she had to confess, she had never been entirely sure she hadn't dreamed the man with the long hair and azure eyes.

But now he sat there, regarding her with polite curiosity, and nothing had ever been more real. He was wearing a sleeveless floor-length robe of some soft homespun material, open over a bare chest and thigh-length short pants that appeared to be constructed of butter-soft leather. He wore Roman sandals on his feet and absolutely nothing else. Gillian swallowed hard.

He was the most powerful man she had ever seen. Even sitting, even relaxed, even doing nothing more than looking at her, he exuded an aura of command and potency that was unnerving. His physique was only a part of it. Strong legs lightly covered with blond-brown hair, muscular thighs, corded abdomen, broad chest, rocklike biceps—these seemed almost incidental to the real strength of the man.

His hair was pulled back and tied at the nape with a leather thong, but Gillian remembered every detail of his face. The broad forehead, the strong Roman nose, the square jaw and full lips...the sky-blue eyes. Perhaps it was in the eyes alone—sharp, quick, yet as unfathomable as a bottomless pool. Those eyes could draw a woman into his arms, helpless with yearning, for the sake of no more than the promise she imagined she saw there. Or send a strong man backing away with no more than a glance. Those eyes could burn with passion to make the world spin or freeze blood to ice. They were the eyes of a man who could command armies or paint masterpieces or build soaring cathedrals, and when Gillian looked into them she saw forever.

She looked at him, and she saw a man...but so much more.

Her impressions of him were so strong, so disorienting, that they left her breathless, and for the first few moments she literally couldn't speak. When she finally regained her senses, she felt like a schoolgirl who had accidentally stumbled into the private room of the football quarterback on whom she had a crush—all blushes and stammers, without a coherent thought in her head. Determinedly she fought for dignity.

"I'm sorry, I didn't mean to— You must be Malik."

He said nothing. Those eyes seemed to go through her, examining her piece by piece. She could feel her cheeks grow warmer.

When she couldn't stand the silence any longer, she said, "I'm Gillian Aldair. Phillipe has been . . ." But she let the words trail off with a vague gesture of apology. If he did not know who she was and that Phillipe had been taking care of her, it was certainly not her place to tell him.

She cast about rather desperately for something to say that would not earn her an immediate escort to the door.

Finally she blurted, "I understand you like van Gogh."

The very slightest lift of his eyebrow expressed his interest—or perhaps amusement—and he replied, "I understand you like coffee. Will you have some?" He lifted his hand toward the silver service on his left.

His voice was deep and rich, with the faintest hint of a Continental accent. The sound of it, as well as the mundanity of the words he spoke, filled Gillian with a profound relief. He was human. He wasn't a figment of her imagination. He wasn't going to draw and quarter her or feed her to the lions or even throw her out of his room. He was, in fact, behaving in a far more gentlemanly fashion than she might have done if their positions had been reversed. She relaxed, though not much.

"I— Um, yes. Thank you."

He made no attempt to pour, so Gillian stepped forward and picked up the heavy urn herself. The cups that surrounded it were bone china set in silver filigree holders, and she filled two.

"I hope it is to your liking," he said. "I haven't had the occasion to drink coffee in many years."

She sipped the hot brew, which was, in fact, a little bitter, and smiled. "It's very nice."

He nodded. "I'll see that you're served some every morning."

He was even more disturbing in close proximity than he had been on first glance—but Gillian supposed anyone would be a little flustered by a body like his, half-naked, sitting less than three feet away. She quickly lowered her eyes to her cup, then looked around for a chair that wasn't too close.

That was not a problem. The room was not designed for cozy conversational groups, and the only other sitting area was a low couch drawn up between two tall bookcases on the opposite wall. The other alternative was a low wooded stool about six feet away from him. She perched on the stool gingerly and sipped her coffee.

"I didn't mean to intrude," she said, gradually regaining her composure. "I wanted to thank you for all you've done."

He did not reply.

"You've been very generous."

Still nothing.

"It was you who rescued me, wasn't it?"

A small incline of his head was her only answer. His silence ate through her equilibrium like acid through plastic. His gaze, steady and absorbing, seemed determined to unravel every thought in her head.

She tried a different tack. "Malik—that's a Muslim name, isn't it?" Language was her subspeciality, and she could only hope to impress him into a reply. "Meaning master?"

She was successful, at least partially. Though his expression did not alter, he answered, "Is it?"

She nodded, trying to relax. "Is that your first name or last?"

He replied, "I have many names. But I think you may call me..." a small smile suggested a joke she didn't understand "...Gabriel."

"Oh." She dropped her eyes to her cup again, inexplicably awkward. She took another sip to calm her nerves. She had dined at the White House, she had made cocktail party conversation with kings and ministers and sat at tables in countries where a slip in protocol could mean imprisonment—and not once had she been as nervous as she was at this moment.

"He was an angel, you know."

She looked up, startled. "Who?"

He made a graceful, deprecating gesture with his hand. "Gabriel. Though I should perhaps say *is* an angel, as angels by definition are given to longevity, aren't they?"

She couldn't help smiling. He was enchanting, in the true old-fashioned sense of the word *enchantment,* meaning to be held under a spell. To be acted upon by magic. Enraptured.

"Yes," she murmured, and she took another sip of the coffee to clear her head. "Yes, I suppose they are."

But she was determined not to leave here without getting some answers—or at least asking the questions. She fortified herself to resist his charm and meet his gaze again, to endure its nerve-tingling intensity for as long as she had to.

"You have an incredible place here," she said. "It brings up a lot of questions, though."

He chuckled softly. "I imagine it does."

His laughter, soft and brief though it was, was reassuring. Encouraged, she went on. "For example—"

But he interrupted, "Tell me about you, Gillian Aldair."

Gillian was taken aback for a moment, not so much by the request as by the way in which it was issued—like an order. But she was the one who had repaid the man's hospitality by sneaking into his room in the middle of the night and invading his privacy. She was hardly in a position to take offense. Besides, it was only fair—she would answer his questions; he would answer hers.

She drew a breath, trying to relax on the uncomfortable stool, "I'm an anthropologist. I teach in a small university in the Midwest. My father is Corning Aldair, of the United States Senate." She hated herself for doing that, but sometimes a little judicious name-dropping could be helpful...just in case. "My husband is—was—a doctor, but he died two years ago. I've always used my maiden name," she added by way of explanation.

She thought she saw his glance flicker to her hand, where she still wore the wedding ring, but it was too quick to be sure. His words were polite, nothing more. "I'm sorry for your loss."

Her throat tightened, as it did every time sympathy was offered, even if the sentiment came from an insincere stranger. The constriction made her tone a little curt as she answered, "Thank you."

He said nothing more, but leaned back in his chair and, steepling his two index fingers together and resting them just below his lips, settled back to listen...and to watch.

In a moment Gillian was able to continue in a more casual manner. "Anyway, I haven't really been in the field in a long time. My colleagues and I have been researching a so-called 'lost tribe' in this area for some time now. Last year they uncovered the site of what looked to be an ancient temple—the first real evidence we've had that the tribe ever even existed. So this year they asked me to come back with them, and naturally I couldn't refuse. We'd been working all season without making much real progress, when I uncovered a series of petroglyphs that seemed to suggest the real seat of the civilization—the city, if you will—was farther up the mountain.

"It was a reasonable hypothesis," she added, sounding a little defensive even now. "It wasn't all that unusual for temples to be erected outside the perimeter of the city, even some distance from it, and if we're taking the Maya or the Aztecs as our model..." She caught herself, and was both amazed and embarrassed at having gotten so carried away.

She had barely even thought about what had brought her here until now, yet in less than five minutes with this stranger she was reexperiencing all the passion for her work that had gotten her back into the field in the first place. And she had a great many more important concerns at the moment than lost tribes, no matter how ancient.

"At any rate," she admitted, "there was a certain amount of debate—disagreement actually. We were only scheduled to be here another week and we'd wasted a lot of time arguing. The team leader insisted there was nothing to justify our going any farther up the mountain. The rest of them wanted to take the data back and study it, but I couldn't wait a whole year to find out, even assuming we were allowed to come back next season. One thing I've learned recently is that life is never certain. So I set off to find out for myself what was up the trail—if anything."

"Impetuous of you, don't you think?"

"I suppose." She sipped her coffee. "But I came here to do a job and I saw no reason to do it halfway. Besides, I was curious. And I didn't intend to be gone more than one night. But of course the landslide changed that."

"So it did." Still he sat in that thoughtful, relaxed pose, his fingers touching his lips, watching her with an easy, alert interest that made Gillian want to squirm in her seat.

She knew she could not take much more of this. She squared her shoulders and prepared to face the issue head-on.

"Are you the one who operated on me?"

He inclined his head once. "I am."

She released a pent-up breath cautiously. "Then you're a doctor."

She did not like the small hesitation before he nodded.

She drew another breath. "I had a broken leg and ribs, is that right? Among other things?"

Again he nodded.

"But Phillipe says I've only been here a few days." She tried to force a laugh but could barely manage a weak smile. "Now, you and I both know that's impossible."

"Wounds heal very quickly here."

"That's ridiculous!" She sprang to her feet and angrily put the coffee cup aside. Until that moment she had not realized how much she had counted on him to put a logical spin on everything she didn't understand, to make sense of the insanity. But if he was going to play these stupid games, as well ...

Or maybe they weren't games. Maybe he was only telling what he believed to be the truth. Maybe he was crazy. Maybe she was. Maybe wounds *did* heal more quickly here. Miracles were being discovered in the rain forests every day; why not in the mountains, as well?

Because it was ridiculous, that was why. Something very weird was going on here, and she was determined to find out what it was.

She crossed the room and pretended to admire a small dark portrait of a woman in Elizabethan dress, using the time to modulate her voice and bring her frustration under control. She could feel his eyes watching her, calmly, assessingly.

"It's lovely," she said in a moment, indicating the portrait.

"Yes," he agreed. "She was."

"Where is this place?" she asked. "I haven't seen any windows."

"That's because we're inside a mountain. An extinct volcano, actually."

She stared at him. "But how ... ?" The immensity of her question outstripped words. How had he

managed it, how could he afford it, how had he
transported building materials? How could he sup-
ply water and power and the kind of high-tech
equipment it would take to run an operating room
capable of supporting the kind of surgery she had
undergone? Where did the food come from, where
did the *people* come from, how could he live like this,
why would he want to?

No, it was impossible.

Reading the expression on her face, he answered
at least one of her questions with a simple under-
statement. "It's very private."

Gillian turned away, closing her eyes briefly and
pressing her palms together as though holding on to
her sanity by force. Impossible, she assured herself.
Her team had thoroughly mapped out the area, their
guides had confirmed the barrenness. There were no
people living in this part of the Andes, not even Indians. There were no structures, and as for this entire complex having been built underground—why,
the mobilization of technology required would have
made headlines for weeks. No one could accomplish
something like this in secret, and they surely would
have heard about it—if only in the form of rumors
or legends—when they set out to explore this part of
the mountains.

Or perhaps they had. Perhaps the lore they had
associated with the lost tribe of ancient times was
really connected, somehow, to a more modern legend. To this place. This man.

But no. It was all too complicated, too convoluted, and how was she supposed to think at all with those eyes boring into her back, stripping her down, drinking her in like cool wine?

"You really are a lovely woman, aren't you?"

The sound of his voice startled her, as did the words themselves, murmured thoughtfully, assessingly, as though it were a conclusion he had come to after studying the matter at length. Gillian shot a quick glance at him. He remained seated, his gaze still fixed upon her with reflective interest.

"Your face, your hair, your figure..."

As he spoke, his eyes moved over her with approval and appreciation, making Gillian's skin tingle uncomfortably.

"All quite exquisite, really. And not something one would expect in a lady explorer." He returned his gaze to her face and added curiously, "Or perhaps it is de rigueur these days for females to take on men's roles without sacrificing their femininity. An altogether satisfactory state of affairs, I'd say."

There was a great deal to pick up on in that, but Gillian only wanted to change the subject. She was far too uncertain of herself—and of him—to enjoy being the object of this stranger's sexual interest.

She picked up a small fat statue carved of rough stone. "Pre-Columbian?"

"Oriental, actually."

She heard the faint creak of wood and rustle of clothing as he rose, and every muscle in her body tensed in expectation of his approach.

"I think your name should have been Pandora." Lazy amusement underscored his voice. "Although even she did not ask so many questions."

"It's my nature to be curious," Gillian replied, carefully replacing the statue on the shelf. Her heartbeat had increased its pace, and even the hairs on the back of her arms prickled as she sensed his nearness. "Also what makes me so good at my job."

"Ah," he said softly. "But do you work all the time?"

He was standing close to her now, inches away, all maleness and muscles and subtle body heat. Her skin responded to him, her nerves responded to him; the tempo of her pulse and the dryness of her throat and the pace of her breathing were all in response to him.

She knew if she looked at him her face would reveal her vulnerability to his nearness, yet she felt like a coward for refusing to face him. She tried, therefore, for a compromise. She did not move away, and she kept her voice casual and detached—admirably so, under the circumstances—as she replied, "Most of the time, yes. And you really can't just present me with a situation as bizarre as this and not expect me to ask a few questions, now can you?"

Then, and only then, did she feel confident enough to step away—casually, pretending to examine another piece of bric-a-brac on the shelf. Almost immediately she began to breathe easier.

There was amusement in his tone as he replied, "Ask as many questions as you like. We have nothing but time to answer them all."

She seized on the opportunity to distract him—and herself. "Your house," she said, gesturing expansively. "It's magnificent. All these treasures. I was thinking this afternoon it's like a fairy tale."

Now she ventured to glance at him, and saw his lips curve in an indulgent smile. Though the smile gentled his features and made him seem far less intimidating than he had been a moment ago, his sex appeal was only heightened. "I'm glad it pleases you."

She swallowed, clearing her throat and forcing a smile. "It's like nothing I've ever seen. Of course, I don't see how you can live without windows."

He took a step forward; that was all it took to close the distance between them. Before Gillian could turn away, or even want to do so, he reached up and gently took her face between his hands. His touch washed through her veins, flooding her senses with his strength and nearness. Her heart began to pound, slow and steady.

"Ah," he said softly, "but you can see heaven from my bed."

Slowly he tilted her head back until her eyes were free of the mesmeric force of his, then farther back until her gaze focused on the ceiling. The ceiling was high, and done in tiers for a three-dimensional effect. On the first tier was painted a magnificent depiction of a night sky studded with brilliant stars. That gave way to an inner tier that represented a close-up view of the stars and planets that comprised the stars. And beyond that was an artist's concept of heaven that was worthy of Michelangelo, complete with winged cherubim, cerulean clouds and alabaster angels. The effect was breathtaking, overwhelming and at least as disturbing as the man who stood so close to her now, holding her face between his strong hands.

When Gillian turned her head to look at him, he let his fingers slide from her cheeks to the back of her neck, cupping her head, fingers threading through her hair. She could see the slow rise and fall of his chest where his robe parted over powerful breast muscles, and the strong cords of his neck. His face was a mere breath away from hers; his heat infused her, and she could see the small shadowed pores of his skin where his beard had been shaved away. Her heart was pounding so hard it hurt her stomach; she was sure he could see her chest shake with the force of it.

"Who *are* you?" she whispered hoarsely.

His eyes were deep with passion, the color of a Caribbean ocean a hundred feet down. His index finger traced the curve of her ear, his thighs brushed hers. He answered softly, "Your dream come true."

He was going to kiss her. She saw his eyes lower, his mouth drift toward hers. She could taste his breath, feel his power. She felt like Persephone in Hades, knowing one taste could condemn her forever, but lacking the will to resist . . . and then suddenly, unexpectedly, finding the courage to do so.

She did not try to break away. She held her stance and held his gaze, yet the steadiness of her voice surprised her as she replied, "Or my worst nightmare."

He stopped. A slow smile curved his lips that deepened with appreciation as he raised his eyes to her again. His hands caressed her neck, but it was a departing, regretful stroke rather than a seductive one. "I shall try very hard not to be that."

His hands drifted down over her shoulders, lightly shaping her arms, the indentation of her waist, barely brushing the curve of her hips. Gillian's skin tingled and her nerves flared with heat and awareness along the course of his touch. But she held her ground.

"I would like to go back to my room now," she said firmly.

He stepped back politely. "I shall be sorry to see you go."

Her heart continued to pound. It was all she could do to keep her breathing steady. "Good night."

"Good night, Gillian Aldair," he replied. "I'm very glad you found me."

His smile followed her across the room, out the door and through the corridor. It even followed her into her dreams.

# Chapter Three

Gillian awoke the next morning strongly tempted to declare everything that had happened the night before nothing more than a dream. This place could not be what it appeared to be. The works of art and antiquities had to be nothing more than clever copies. Her injuries had obviously not been as serious as she had thought. But that man...Gabriel... She could not explain him away so easily.

A dream? Hardly. She could still feel his breath on her skin, the press of his hand against her neck. His fingers, long and strong as they threaded through her hair. The swell of his chest muscles, the width of his neck, the flatness of his stomach. Those blazing blue eyes. An eccentric millionaire, a rock star living out some bizarre fantasy, a madman, nature's most perfect male specimen—he might be any of those or all four. But he definitely was no dream.

Just how she could be sure it was morning in the windowless room, she wasn't sure. There was an iridescent light source that came from behind frost glass panes in the ceiling which seemed to mimic skylight. The light that came through them was soft and indirect, suggesting morning, as it was no doubt meant to. The little crystal lamps and sconces she had noticed last night were unlighted, and the supper tray had been removed.

Gillian pushed back the covers and slid out of bed. She jerked down the hem of her nightgown and deliberately ignored the temptation to reexamine the scar, or to look for others. The answer to her most pressing question had quietly occurred to her, as seemingly unsolvable problems often do, while she had slept. It was really very simple: she had experienced a memory loss.

The last thing she remembered of the landslide was Gabriel's rescue. Obviously he had found a way to get her airlifted out, and she had spent the next several months in a hospital or extended-care facility. She had had a head injury and was suffering from selective amnesia regarding those months. It was even possible that her amnesia had been more extensive, and that, until she had told him last night, Gabriel did not know who she was or whom to contact about her injuries. But whether he was a physician or a humanitarian—or something far, far less noble— he had brought her here, to his hideaway beneath the mountain, to recover.

As for where "here" might be... She looked around the room.

It truly was palatial. She had been far too concerned with other things yesterday to give it the attention it deserved, but now she looked around with awe. The muted light added a subtle fairy-tale quality that Gillian found particularly suited to her surroundings.

The floor beneath her feet was fashioned of glazed ceramic tiles in a lovely blue-and-white starburst pattern, accented now and then by plush Aubusson carpets in muted roses and greens. The ceiling was a pastel mural of a summer sky graced with floating cherubs and nearly transparent angels. The delicate furniture was upholstered in candy-colored silks—yellow, strawberry and mint—and decorated with lavish gilding. On every polished surface was a profusion of art, fine sculptures, crystal vases and framed needlework that had a distinctly antique air.

The silk walls provided the perfect backdrop for a collection of mirrors and paintings hung from velvet ribbons. In addition to the van Gogh she had noticed yesterday, one appeared to be a Renoir. Yet another was signed by an artist who claimed to be Matisse.

One had to be just a little in awe of a man who would furnish his guest quarters with paintings by Renoir. On the other hand, Gillian did not know too many people whose guest quarters were roughly the size of the average suburban home. Why shouldn't such a place be furnished like a room in the Louvre?

She found a palatial bathroom with a sunken tub big enough to swim in. Silent servants had laid out towels, jasmine-scented bath salts and a colorful gauze shift for her to wear. When she emerged from the tub, more smiling servants were waiting to attend to her every need. Gillian found all this attention somewhat disconcerting, though she had to admit there was a part of her that enjoyed being indulged after weeks of wilderness living.

She caught a glimpse of her reflection in a mirrored wall as they moved back toward the bedroom, and she couldn't help being pleased with what she saw. The deep purple garment complemented her dark hair and brown eyes, and the way it billowed and swirled when she moved was charmingly feminine. Her cheeks had a healthy glow she had no reason to expect, and the dark pockets that had outlined her eyes—caused by too little sleep and too much squinting over poorly drawn maps by lantern light—had almost completely disappeared. She looked as though she had spent the last week in a health spa, and except for a lingering tenderness in her leg and a few aching muscles, she felt as though she had, too. She felt, in fact, better than she had in a long, long time—which was only one of the reasons it was hard to believe that only a few days ago she had been lying trapped under a half ton of mountain, waiting to die.

That was the problem, of course. She wasn't sure *what* she believed anymore.

Her breakfast tray contained yet another banquet of assorted delicacies—and a porcelain carafe of fresh coffee. She sat down to enjoy herself, determined to seek Gabriel out as soon as she finished.

As it happened, she didn't have to. She had barely finished her first fruit muffin, and was trying to decide which of the creamy soft cheeses to try with the next, when he appeared at her open door. She almost choked on her coffee.

He was wearing a flowing white shirt open at the collar and tucked into tight black trousers that reminded her of a bygone age. Tall black leather boots completed the outfit. His hair was combed back from his forehead and fell loose around his shoulders; the hint of a smile curved his full lips. He was enough to stop the heart of any red-blooded woman in midbeat.

*Rock star,* Gillian thought dazedly. *Definitely a multimillionaire rock star.*

"Good morning, Gillian," he said. The rich timbre of his voice brought a delicious tingle to her spine, and she loved the way his accent softened and rolled the syllables of her name. "May I join you?"

Gillian gestured to the seat opposite her at the small lace-covered table. "Please."

She tried not to be obvious, but she couldn't help watching him as he crossed the room. He moved fluidly, with the supple grace of a jungle animal, easy and natural. The clothing he wore took her back to an earlier, more romantic era, flattering his form and bringing the pure maleness of him into sharp focus. Gillian could see it was going to be very difficult to maintain the polite yet remote attitude that she had decided would be appropriate with him.

His smile was knowing and approving as he reached her. "So you do find me attractive. That's good."

Gillian was almost too taken aback to react. She swallowed hard and quickly averted her eyes, picking up her coffee cup. "Actually, I was just noticing your boots." She managed to keep her voice cool. "I think this must be the first time I've seen anyone here wear shoes."

He pulled out a chair. "There's hardly any need. The floors are heated and smooth to walk on. However, the last I recall it was considered uncivilized to dine in one's bare feet. Am I right? Or have times changed since I was last outside? They often do."

She stared at him. "Since you were outside?"

He sat across from her and helped himself to a piece of fruit from the basket. "How is the coffee?"

"It's strong," she admitted, though she didn't want to seem ungrateful. "Would you like some?"

He hesitated, then smiled. "Perhaps I will. It's been a long time since I've tasted it, or even wanted to. But I think I will enjoy being corrupted by you."

There were four charmingly decorated stoneware mugs on the tray with the coffee carafe; he reached forward and filled one for himself.

"Is there anything else you would like, Gillian?" he inquired as he settled back again. "Are you comfortable here?"

She refused to be defeated by his solicitousness. She would remain polite but firm, though the detachment she had hoped for was becoming increasingly difficult to maintain. Every time he said her name, rolling the word off his tongue with a lyrical rhythm vaguely suggestive of intimacy, she lost a little more of it.

She sat up straighter in her chair and pretended she was addressing a foreign dignitary—the minister of antiquities in a country in which she had applied to dig, perhaps. She was a guest and, as such, dependent upon his generosity, but at the same time she mustn't let him forget she had power of her own. It was a role she had played many times. What surprised her was how easy it was to imagine Gabriel in the opposite role—minister or king, ruler of nations.

She wondered then if he might be some third-world prince, exiled or in hiding from assassins. He did not have a Middle Eastern look, but there were a number of small nations to whom the age of technology had brought sudden, immense wealth.

With an effort she resisted the temptation to speculate further, and answered his question. "You've been more than kind. But if it's not too much trouble, there are a couple of things I need."

He tilted his head in gracious inquiry.

"I'd like to have my old clothes back, if you don't mind."

He lifted an eyebrow. "You don't like the gowns the women make?"

"They're beautiful, of course." The one Gillian was wearing today was a deep grape color, almost luscious enough to eat, and as soft as silk against her skin. She fingered the folds appreciatively. "But I'm used to something a little more practical."

"That is practical for here."

She had no argument for that. "Nonetheless, I'd be more comfortable in my own clothes."

He tore off the corner of a piece of nutty bread, holding it between his fingers for a moment as he explained, "We had to cut your clothes off you. I'm afraid there wasn't much to salvage. However, I'm sure we can put together a wardrobe you'll find more suitable. I'll put the women on it right away."

"Oh." She tried to push the picture of her own body, so badly mangled her clothing had to be cut away, out of her mind. "Thank you."

He popped the piece of bread into his mouth, watching as she regained her composure. It didn't take her long.

"But that's really one of the other things I wanted to talk to you about," she said, picking up her coffee cup. "All these servants—I'm not used to people watching me bathe and helping me dress and hovering over me with dishes of candy and cool drinks and steaming towels in case I want to wash my hands. I mean, really. Half the time I feel like I'm in some kind of harem."

The smile that deepened one corner of his lips brought a playfully wicked spark to his eyes. "What makes you think you're not?"

Gillian was a little alarmed to discover she couldn't be sure he was teasing. She took a sip of her coffee, forcing nonchalance into her expression. "I'll add it to my list," she said.

He picked up her coffee cup, still smiling. "They're not servants, as a matter of fact. They simply live here, just as I do. Generosity and solicitude are considered virtues in their culture, and if they hover over you it's because you fascinate them. Not many people from the outside come here."

He sipped from the cup, grimaced slightly and put it down. "That is a vile brew, isn't it? I can't see why you like it."

Gillian smiled. "I don't want to offend anyone. If it makes the women happy to wait on me, please don't hurt their feelings. I'm just not used to it, that's all."

There were, of course, a dozen questions swirling in her head based on his comments—who these people were, why they lived here, what their culture was, why there was no record of their existence here—but he did not give her a chance to ask them, and it was probably for the best. She didn't really want to get involved in a long conversation with him...did she?

"You are my guest and I won't have you made to feel uncomfortable," he said with a dismissive wave of his hand. "I will speak to the women. Is there anything else?"

She took a breath, trying at the same time to make her voice casual, her request perfectly reasonable. "I'd like to use your radio, please. I need to contact my base camp."

His expression was grave. "I'm sorry to tell you your friends are gone. They searched diligently for you but were forced to abandon their efforts when they came upon the landslide. They found the body of your companion and must have assumed you were buried beneath the rubble."

Gillian stared at him, trying to adjust to the news which shouldn't, after all, have been surprising to her. Of course they wouldn't search forever, or wait for her to show up at camp against all odds. Their permissions to dig had almost expired, and so had their supplies. They would go back to Lima to regroup, notify the authorities and return with more searchers and supplies. They wouldn't just assume she was dead. They would continue to look until they found some evidence of what had become of her. Wouldn't they?

She swallowed hard, clearing her throat. "Then I need to contact Lima. I can leave a message for my friends there."

He bit into a mango, sharp white teeth neatly severing the section and disposing of it. Gillian had never before realized that watching a man eat could be a sensual experience.

"That would be impossible, I'm afraid. There is no radio." He bit into the mango again. She stared at him.

"You have to have a radio," she insisted with forced, deliberate calm. "No one would live way out here—wherever here is—without some way to communicate with the outside world. What if there was an emergency?"

He seemed intrigued by that possibility. "What kind of emergency?"

Gillian found herself momentarily at a loss. What kind of emergency, indeed? The kind wherein they found an American woman crushed by a landslide and near death? Apparently no outside help had been needed to remedy that situation. Fire, flood, natural disaster? If they were, indeed, inside a mountain—which she still wasn't sure she believed—it seemed unlikely any of those things could threaten their existence here and even more unlikely that a radio call to the outside world would prevent it.

But stubbornly she persisted. "What about a cellular phone? Surely with all these luxuries—" she gestured expansively around the room "—you've found a way to hook up a telephone relay." The sarcasm that backed her tone was induced by desperation. "Not even a hermit would be caught without his fax machine these days."

He looked amused. "What is that?"

She blinked. "Fax machine? You know, a facsimile transmitter...." And she stopped, eyes narrowing. "How long have you been here, anyway?"

He tore off another chunk of dark nut bread and spread it lavishly with cheese. "And that other thing you said—cellular phone? This differs from the telephone how?"

She said carefully, "It's portable. It doesn't have to be hard-wired for reception. You can take it practically anywhere in the world...."

"Not here, I'm afraid." He smiled and took a bit out of the bread. "But what an interesting concept."

He leaned back in his chair, a thoughtful, pleased look coming into his eyes as he looked at her. "You have a great deal to teach me, I see. And it surprises me to find how much I'm looking forward to learning. What a genuine treasure you've turned out to be!"

Gillian's head was clamoring with so many questions she couldn't even sort them out to voice one, and her emotions were equally tangled. Amazement, curiosity and disbelief warred with suspicion and worry, and all were overlaid with the odd vulnerability any woman feels when an attractive man says flattering things about her.

The only weapon with which Gillian had to defend herself was her dignity, and she clung to it stubbornly. She picked up her coffee cup and replied coolly, "I certainly hope you don't intend to add me to your collection."

"If I did," he assured her with all due sincerity, "you would without question be the jewel in my crown."

Gillian swallowed her coffee and returned the mug to the table carefully. "I need to get a message to Lima. I have to contact my colleagues and let them know I'm all right. They'll send transportation back for me."

"Oh, I really doubt they could find the place." His attitude was infuriatingly unconcerned as his strong fingers tore apart an orange, exposing the lush ripe fruit within.

Gillian struggled to keep her tone reasonable. "Then perhaps you would be good enough to loan me a jeep—"

"A what?" Again that look of quick curiosity lightened his eyes.

"Or a snowsled or a skateboard or a camel, for heaven's sake, or whatever you people use for transportation in this little corner of Oz!" She abandoned her efforts to remain composed, and her voice grew shrill. She gripped the edge of the table to keep from leaping out of her seat at him. "Good God, what kind of man has never heard of a *jeep*, anyway?"

He tossed a scrap of orange peel onto his plate. "I've heard of it. But what makes you think I would have an army vehicle on the premises, I can't imagine. Skateboard, however—now, that's something I don't believe I'm familiar with. You'll have to tell me about it later.''

But then he smiled, and it was the kind of smile to make Gillian wonder just how seriously to take him . . . to make her almost want to relax and forget her suspicions and trust him to take care of everything.

"Gillian," he said gently, "it's a ten-mile hike back down to your campsite, and the landslide has blocked the trail. To go around it would take weeks on the back of a burro, and you know you're not strong enough to make the trip yet. Is your life here so unbearable? Or perhaps—" now a slight deepening of one corner of his lips, the kind of rueful smile designed to melt the female heart "—it is the company?"

There was a certain logic to what he said, she knew that. She was still too weak to undertake the rigors of a trail which would test the endurance of a person in perfect health. The landslide would have only made matters worse. But she tightened her hands in her lap and insisted stubbornly, "I only want to send a message to my friends."

He inclined his head, still smiling gently. "Hardly an unreasonable request. I suppose I shall just have to see what can be arranged, won't I?"

His conciliatory attitude made her previous behavior seem churlish, and she was embarrassed. "I'd appreciate it," she said, a little stiffly. "And I'm sorry if I seemed ungrateful . . . before."

"Then answer my question. Are you so unhappy here?"

Gillian met his eyes squarely and told the absolute truth. "I don't know where *here* is. I don't know who you are or what kind of scam you're running or even what day it is. I don't know whether I'm a guest in a billionaire's mansion or about to be sold into white slavery. *Should* I be happy here?"

He chuckled. Gillian preferred his laughter to the cool penetrating looks she had come to associate with him, but even the twinkle in his blue eyes could not completely erase the cynicism that perpetually lurked there. "I am going to enjoy you," he said.

"And that's another thing," she replied shortly. "I don't particularly like being referred to as though I'm a meal you're looking forward to or a pet you like to indulge."

"I don't mean to offend."

He sounded sincere, but the words came out a little too smoothly for Gillian to be entirely convinced. He disposed of the last section of fruit and wiped his fingers on a napkin. His gaze was interested and speculative—completely harmless, she was sure, but a little unnerving nonetheless.

"You have every right to be uneasy, of course. You've survived a major accident and been suddenly torn apart from your associates and completely cut off from the world that's familiar to you.

You've been thrust into this place through no desire of your own, and though we've tried to make you comfortable, it all no doubt seems very strange."

When he put it like that, Gillian had to feel a little ashamed of herself. He had saved her life, after all. No matter who he was or how he had come to be here, she could never overlook the fact that, without him, she would have surely died in the landslide.

Then he went on, "However, I would have thought a woman like yourself would find plenty to keep herself occupied in such a place. What happened to that much-lauded scientific curiosity of yours? Can you really be thinking of ignoring one of the most fascinating studies in social development you're ever likely to come across?"

She frowned a little, considering this, and noticing it, he smiled. He rose and came around to her side of the table. Resting his hands on the back of her chair as though to pull it out for her, he bent over her, his voice low and seductive in her ear. "You may never get another chance like this, Gillian. You know you have a thousand questions. Let me answer them. Let me be your guide on the most exciting adventure you will ever have."

The timbre of his voice, the gentle brush of his breath across the back of her neck, sent a tingling shiver down her spine she could not ignore. If it were possible to make love to a woman with nothing more than his voice, this man would have been an expert. With an effort, Gillian stiffened herself against it.

"I've asked my questions," she replied, "And I have yet to get a straight answer."

"A little mystery is a healthy thing," he murmured, his lips very close to her ear now—so close she could feel his heat creeping through her skin, seeping into her veins, dancing like sparks of electricity down the column of her spine. "It keeps life interesting, don't you think?"

Gillian braced her hands against the table and pushed up. He stood back politely and held her chair.

"I don't like mysteries," she said flatly. "Never have." She stepped away, and almost immediately her pulse began to settle down. "And sometimes the best way to solve a mystery is to step back and examine it from a distance."

"I don't think you believe that." There was amusement in his voice. "Otherwise you would have taken your data on your lost city back to the classroom to examine, as your colleagues suggested, instead of venturing up a dangerous trail in search of it."

He had her there, as he very well knew. She turned slowly. "Are you suggesting you might have information on the city yourself? Here?"

His smile promised nothing—and everything. "My library is extensive, as you will see. I shouldn't be surprised if you found one or two volumes devoted to the prehistory of this area."

He was a master manipulator. Even if the mystery of this place—of him—had not been compelling, as he knew very well it was, despite her protests to the contrary, she could not resist the opportunity to further the research in her own field. He wanted to tempt her, persuade her, cajole her into *wanting* to stay, and the only thing that puzzled her was why he would go to so much trouble.

She looked at him thoughtfully. "You've just told me there's no radio and no way out of here until the trail is cleared. So I'm stuck here whether I like it or not. What difference can it possibly make to you whether I want to stay?"

His eyes moved over her in a leisurely fashion, not so much a caress as an exploration, gently probing and examining. "You are my guest, Gillian, not my prisoner. Your contentment concerns me very much. Because, you see—" he smiled, bringing his hands to rest very lightly on her shoulders "—you are my adventure, as well. And I had thought I would never have another."

He let his hands drift down her arms, a feather touch that nonetheless warmed her skin and sped her heartbeat. His voice was coaxing and seductive. "Let me show you my world, Gillian. You haven't begun to see it all. Share it with me."

With an effort she held his gaze and kept her voice steady. "Why?"

He dropped his hands and stepped back with a rueful shake of his head. "Must everything be so complex for you? Can't it simply be because I want to show you and you want to see?"

Gillian knew, of course, that nothing was that simple. But she also knew that he was right. He hadn't asked her to sacrifice her firstborn child, merely to allow him to be a gracious host. Maybe she was making everything too complicated.

She looked at him for another moment. "All right, Gabriel. Show me your world. And while you're at it, maybe you won't mind answering a few questions."

He smiled and offered his arm to her. "It will be my greatest pleasure."

Gillian somehow doubted that. Nonetheless she took his arm and allowed him to lead her from the room.

## Chapter Four

Gillian had always considered herself on the high end of the cultural literacy scale. Her studies had taken her all over the world, and what she had not seen for herself she had read about. But nothing had prepared her for what she saw that day.

By day the corridor itself was a sight to behold. At first she thought they might be in a courtyard, for she could feel fresh-scented air moving against her cheek and see pale shadows dancing like clouds in the morning sun. But she quickly realized the sense of light and airiness was created by the tall white marble walls and a ceiling higher than she could see. Graceful lengths of white gauze were draped overhead, billowing slightly in the gentle movement of a forced air system. It was all really quite lovely.

The library of which Gabriel was so justifiably proud was a vast vaulted room with so many chambers she did not even begin to explore them all. The main room featured soaring dark oak and spiral staircases that reminded her of an ancient cathedral; exquisite stained glass backlit by an artificial source completed the churchlike effect.

Her eyes easily lit upon a first-edition Shakespeare, a Gutenberg Bible and what appeared to be an original Chaucer. There were manuscripts in Latin, beautifully illuminated in scarlets and gold, lying out in the open for anyone to touch. Gillian hardly dared breathe on them. One case, sensibly glassed, contained a collection of scrolls made of some kind of animal skin, and though her scientist's heart began to pound at the sight of them, she refused to take the responsibility for opening that case.

And along with these volumes, which would have made any museum curator in the world drool shamelessly, were relatively ordinary collections by Defoe and Mark Twain, Dickens and Faulkner and Proust. There were volumes on history, medicine, science and the law—most of them in languages Gillian could not read. There were atlases and maps, many of them hand drawn, dating back to before the discovery of America, which Gillian found fascinating.

The artwork that softened the rich, age-darkened wood walls was at least as impressive. In rapid succession, Gabriel pointed out paintings by Degas, Vermeer and Titian, and he seemed pleased when she recognized the names. Gillian was no art expert by any means, but she had no doubt the paintings were as authentic as the illuminated manuscripts and neatly tied scrolls.

*He's a drug dealer,* she thought dazedly. *Mr. Gabriel Malik is one of those crazy South American drug lords who's built himself a little hideaway here in the Andes... and who has very discriminating taste.*

But she couldn't help wondering if there were enough drugs in the whole world to support a lifestyle like this.

Farther along the corridor was a sauna formed by a natural hot spring that bubbled right out of the stone floor. There was a big banquet hall decorated in the Renaissance style and a kitchen where smiling brown-skinned women urged her with words she did not understand to try their latest confections. The ovens appeared to be built into the stone walls, and Gillian could not determine what power source they used.

She saw a playground, a music room—with instruments she did not begin to recognize—an aviary whose colorful inhabitants made her laugh out loud with delight, and a solarium lush with roses and orchids of every description. Nowhere did she see a telephone or electric outlet. Or a refrigerator or a television or even a shortwave radio. None of the trappings of modern civilization seemed to be present, though all the conveniences were.

This Gabriel Malik, whoever he was, had not just built himself a hideaway in the mountains. He had built a whole civilization.

They took a corridor that was unfamiliar to Gillian, leaving behind the billowing gauze ceiling and gentle light for the smooth stone walls and ambient light whose source was indeterminate. It was like leaving a hotel suite for the service stairs—which, she supposed, was precisely what they had done.

She asked him about the power source.

"Thermoelectric, for the most part," he replied. "Didn't I mention we were inside a volcano?"

She cast him a skeptical look. "I'm still reserving judgment on that."

"And why is that?"

"Because it would have taken an army of engineers a lifetime's work just to tunnel out what I've seen so far, for one thing," she replied immediately. "And that's assuming they could get the equipment in here to do it, which they couldn't. For another, I just can't picture the Peruvian government selling off volcanoes to private individuals, when it took my colleagues three years to even get permission to dig here. And frankly, no matter what else you might have managed to pull off to create your own little piece of paradise, I simply can't believe that you could have the technology and personnel to perform major surgery locked away inside a volcano somewhere."

He cast her an amused and tolerant look. "But you have seen all these things with your own eyes. What a peculiar sense of logic you have."

The corridor had widened into something more like a promenade or a city street. Occasionally they passed other people, most of them dressed in the colorful robes she had grown accustomed to seeing. Children pointed and stared as they passed, grinning in delight; their parents scolded them and shooed them away, smiling friendly broad smiles at Gillian and Gabriel.

"All these people," she murmured. "What do they do?"

"They raise their families, tend their crops, live their lives." He hesitated a moment with thought. "They protect this place."

She looked up at him sharply. "From what?"

He gave a graceful lift of his shoulders which Gillian suspected was not quite as ingenuous as it appeared. "From whatever threatens their home, I suppose."

The corridor appeared to be taking a slight uphill course, and Gillian wondered if they were moving toward an exit of some kind. She cursed herself for not paying more attention to the direction in which they had been walking, but he was considerably more of a distraction than she had counted on. Walking beside him in her flowing purple dress, with her arm tucked securely beneath his, her thoughts tended to drift toward how tall he was, how strong his forearm was and how delicate and feminine he made her feel. It was difficult to remember to look for an escape route.

So far he had been fairly candid with her—to the best of her ability to discern, anyway. Gillian decided to push her luck a little further.

"So," she said with an expansive gesture that was meant to include everything she had, and had not yet, seen. "How can you afford all this, anyway?"

A secretive amusement sparked in his eyes. "That question might be considered rude in some circles."

"Not in mine," she assured him and waited for an answer.

"I'm something of a...collector," he said, choosing his words with obvious care. "Wealth, I've found, is one of the more useful items to collect. And, of course, I have investments."

"Does that mean you are, or are not, a drug dealer?"

The minute she spoke she realized what a stupid thing it was to say, and not just for the obvious reasons. He stopped and turned to look at her, and she felt remorse surge through her even as she blustered to defend herself.

"It's not such an outrageous question," she insisted, squaring her shoulders. "You don't have to look so insulted. It's not as though no one in this part of the world ever made a fortune that way, you know."

But his expression was not so much insulted as curious—and yes, amused. Everything she did seemed to amuse him in one way or another.

"You are a curious child," he observed. "You remind me of a bristling kitten—always trying to make yourself larger when you feel threatened."

She scowled. "I'm not a child."

"And I'm not a drug dealer," he replied equitably. "I'll take your word for it that people do acquire fortunes this way, though the mechanics of it elude me. I personally have no commerce with the outside world."

He offered his arm to her again, but Gillian was a little slow to accept it. "I suppose that must make you a rock star," she murmured after a moment.

He laughed softly. "What peculiar things you say."

"You're a little peculiar yourself."

"That I won't deny."

She glanced up at him to see that the laughter had faded, giving way to a bleak, almost haunted, expression that made Gillian immediately wish she had never spoken. And when he sensed her gaze, he rearranged his expression into something much more bland, leaving her to feel she had been afforded a rare glimpse into the real Gabriel . . . and leaving her more confused than ever about what kind of man he might be.

"Watch your step," he said, moving in front of her. "There are stairs."

He extended his hand backward for her, and she placed her hand in his, grateful for the support as he guided her up the set of spiraling stone stairs that were cut so steeply they reminded her of the pyramids on the Mexican coast.

She said as much to him, huffing a little with exertion, and then added, "I always wondered if the Maya had longer legs than modern man does."

"Actually, no," he replied. "It was a simple matter of engineering. The technology simply didn't exist to—" And then he cut himself off and glanced back at her with a smile. "But I'm lecturing an anthropologist, who already knows all this. You mustn't let me bore you."

Gillian did not think it was humanly possible to ever be bored by anything this man said or did. "You speak with such authority. Are you a student of archaeology?"

"I am a student of many things," he replied. "Come. Look."

He pulled her up the last step and they were standing on a ledge secured by an iron railing, overlooking the most incredible sight Gillian had ever seen.

Below her as far as she could see was green earth—rich cultivated fields, orchards, meadows. Waterfalls tumbled out of the rock walls, sending a soothing whisper up to them, and mist rose from the shimmering blue stream that meandered in and out of the greenery. The colors were misty and muted, rich with shadow and depth, and the quality of the light was entirely different from anything she had seen before. It took Gillian a moment to realize why.

She lifted her head and saw, far above them, the rock walls give way to a ragged circle of blue sky, spilling streams of sunlight down into the tunnel world.

"Oh my." It was a little more than a whisper, and it was all she could manage for a moment.

He said simply, "You said you missed windows."

"But it's like—" She struggled for words, spreading her hands. "It's like something you would see in a movie. How in the world— You couldn't have built this! How is it possible?"

"It's all done with mirrors, you know."

She gave a surprised laugh, but when she looked at him found he was perfectly serious.

"The sunlight," he explained. "It's all funnelled down and magnified with a series of mirrors—much of the interior is lighted in the same way. And, of course, the heat that produces creates the ideal tropical environment for organic agriculture."

She stared at him. He sounded so matter of fact... but why should she doubt him? All he had done was create an artificial environment underground. The idea of the biosphere was hardly a new one, and it was already being proven a viable habitat.

She shook her head in slow wonder. "You are an amazing man. And all this..." She twisted her head around, absorbing the bouncing sunlight, the misty greens, the tumbling stream, the fog that hovered so romantically just above the surface of the ground. "It's more than a fairy tale. I'm not sure I believe any of it, but I'll never forget it. Not ever."

"I'm glad." He smiled, lifting his hand to touch her hair, lightly tucking one strand behind her ear. "Because I find you somewhat amazing, as well. And I have no intention of forgetting you."

His touch upon her hair was a simple gesture, harmless and neutral, but it was the prelude to something more. She saw it in his eyes, felt it with every cell of her body. Her heart began to pound and her breath to quicken, responding to him even before he made a move.

His hands settled lightly on her shoulder, then tightened, pulling her close. She felt the strength of his thighs pressed against hers, the heat from his chest flowing over her. In the soft white sunlight she could see the shadow of muscled arms beneath his shirt, and before she could stop herself, her hands— of their own violation—had lifted to them, fingers spreading over hard biceps.

His fingers teased the curve of her collarbone, caressed the back of her neck. His breath was warm on her cheek, his eyes intent with passion as they followed the movement of his fingers over the curve of her neck, her jaw, the shell of her ear, her face. Gillian's breath felt thunderous and at the same time oxygen-poor; she was dizzy and it was difficult to think. His hand opened on the side of her face, guiding it toward his. He bent his head to her.

Just as she felt the rush of his breath against her parted lips, and with a strength of will that surprised even her, Gillian turned her face away. "Don't," she whispered. It sounded more like a gasp. "Please."

"Ah, Gillian," he murmured. His lips brushed her cheekbone, sending rivulets of heat across the network of her skin. "Not even a kiss? How you disappoint me."

She struggled to recover her breath, to stiffen against his embrace. It was very nearly impossible to do either. "No," she said, as firmly as she could manage. "Not even a kiss."

"I see." He dropped his hands to her shoulders, caressing them lightly. He lowered his eyes and even managed to make his voice sound regretful. "You find me repugnant."

"You know that's not true." She was still breathing hard. With a determined effort, she braced her hands against his forearms and stepped back.

His hands drifted down to her elbows, but even though he was still touching her, still making her body want to respond to him in all sorts of unmanageable ways, the small distance she had managed to put between them allowed her to regain some of her composure.

"I don't know you. I don't trust you. You could be a genius or a madman or a criminal or a saint and

I sometimes think you might be a combination of all of them."

His smile was slow and caressing and infuriatingly seductive. "Is that so terrible?"

"Yes!" She deliberately fueled her indignation, hoping to reinforce her resolve. "You brought me here, you keep me here, you refuse to explain any of it to my satisfaction or even let me communicate with the outside world so *I* can explain it.... You pet and pamper and indulge me, and when you come on to me like that you make me feel as though you're presenting me with a bill! It's—it's unchivalrous!"

At last she seemed to have struck a chord with him. The passion in his eyes, though it did not completely fade, slowly became tinged with understanding. He straightened up, still holding her elbows in a gentle caress and looked at her thoughtfully.

"Ah," he said softly. "I do see. You think I want only to seduce you, to claim your body and know its pleasures. Ah, Gillian, how little you understand me."

His hands stroked upward on her outer arms now, causing a constriction of Gillian's throat, a renewed increase in the pace of her pulse.

"Once when I was young I sought those delicious games of seduction for their own sake. I reveled in women, I inhaled them, I wanted to devour their youth and beauty as though by drawing it inside me I could own it...." His voice was low and passionate, its timbre seeming to reverberate through her skin. But there was sadness in his eyes, the same bleak longing she had noticed so briefly earlier, and it frightened her a little.

As though sensing her disturbance, he softened his expression. His fingers drifted down her arms now and entwined with hers. "As I grow older, however," he said, "I find myself becoming more discriminating, more demanding...for you see, my dear lovely girl, physical pleasures are far too fleeting and shallow, and the virtue that you guard so closely is the thing that is of the least interest to me."

His fingers tightened and his voice grew husky as his eyes darkened with passion. "I want much, much more from you than your company in my bed. I want your mind, your soul, your every thought and wish. I want you to teach me, to make me smile, to make me think. I want to fill myself with you, to get drunk on you, for nothing like you has happened to me in too long to remember."

The torrent of words left her dizzy, intoxicating her in the same way his kisses might have done. His grip on her fingers was strong and warm, his lips and his breath and his body close to her, blending into her, and the fire in his eyes made her blood rush.

Slowly, inch by fraction of an inch, he released the pressure on her hands, and he straightened up. "I want you, Gillian," he said softly. He caressed her cheek once, briefly, and then let his hand fall away. "Make no mistake about that. And eventually we will see heaven together from my bed. When that time will come is yours to choose. And until then—'' he let his hand drop, and took a step back from her ''—I am your servant, and your will is mine to obey.''

Her heart was beating hard and her skin still tingled all over from his touch. She stared at him until she could regain her voice. ''I think,'' she said at last, and only a little hoarsely, ''you could be a dangerous man. I'm a little afraid of you.''

He smiled. ''That's good. Every woman, I think, should be a little afraid of her lover . . . just as every man inevitably fears the woman he loves.'' He offered his arm to her. ''But I've tired you. Come, I'll take you back to your rooms.''

Gillian accompanied him wordlessly, but her head did not stop spinning with the questions and uncertainties until exhaustion finally claimed her far into the night.

# Chapter Five

Gabriel had been aware of Phillipe's presence for some time, but he avoided looking up—perhaps because he knew what the other man was going to say. He had been working all night, just as he did most nights, for he required very little sleep, and his mind was fatigued. He didn't have the patience for Phillipe this morning.

Phillipe, on the other hand, was fully capable of standing there, waiting to be acknowledged, all day and into the night if he had to.

Gabriel placed a drop of solution in the fixative, then ran it through the scanner. He was researching the properties of a hybrid he had created from high-altitude lichen and a seventh-generation genetically altered cacao plant. Absently he wondered if this would make him the "drug dealer" Gillian seemed to suspect him of being. Before she arrived, he had been acutely involved in this work, but now it was only a way to pass the hours until he could see her again. And that, no doubt, would only be added to Phillipe's list of complaints if he knew about it.

"What is it, Phillipe?" he said, selecting another specimen vial.

The little man shifted his weight once, from foot to foot, and his troubled frown remained firmly fixed in place. "It is not good, Malik," he said. "You know it's not."

Gabriel did not look up, giving his attention, such as it was, to his work. "I've asked you not to call me that. My name is Gabriel now."

The frown deepened a fraction. "That's difficult to remember."

"It's a fine, solid Anglo-Saxon name. There was an angel named Gabriel, you know."

"I know."

"Malik is a Muslim name, did you know that? It means 'master.' Completely unsuitable for this day and age, don't you think?"

"If you say so. The matter of names is of very little importance to me at the moment."

Resigned, Gabriel looked up at him. "And what is important to you, Phillipe? What is it that's not good?"

"The woman. She should be with her own people. She can only bring trouble here, and the people—the protectors—are worried."

Gabriel looked at him steadily, but not unkindly. "Don't you mean you're worried?"

"Legend tells of wars being fought to protect this place."

"There were no wars," Gabriel replied tiredly.

"Of spies who have come and died for their efforts," Phillipe continued unfazed. "That is why the protectors were formed, all those generations ago, to keep the secrets of this place. It is a heritage they will not forget. They don't *want* to forget."

Gabriel frowned. "That is a useless and outdated custom. Times have changed. The protectors have no function anymore. Their title is only honorary, you know that."

"You will not convince them of that, Malik," Phillipe said soberly. "The woman—she is welcome here as your consort and will be loved by the people if she wishes to be. But what will happen if she does not wish to stay?"

Fire flashed in Gabriel's eyes. "That is absurd!"

He pushed abruptly out of his chair, a movement that might have been interpreted as threatening by someone who knew him less well. Phillipe stood his ground, his expression calm.

"Why should she not want to stay?" Gabriel demanded angrily. "Haven't I given her every luxury she could ask for? Haven't I put my rarest treasures at her disposal, opened up every chamber of this place to her, given orders that her smallest wish is to be fulfilled without delay? What could she possibly lack?"

And then the thunderstorm in his eyes sharpened into dark suspicion. "Has she spoken to you? Tell me, what has she said?"

"She has said nothing of her discontent to me."

"Then she *has* no discontent!" Gabriel replied shortly.

He made an abrupt dismissive gesture and turned back to his worktable, scowling. "You are a foolish old man. Return to your duties and cease your troublesome gossip."

Phillipe acknowledged the dismissal with a respectful nod of his head and turned toward the door. But he could not resist adding, one more time, "She should have been returned to her people before she awoke."

When he was once again alone, Gabriel abandoned any pretense of interest in his work. His interest in anything was noticeably short-lived these days, his passions even shorter...for everything, that was, except Gillian. And that was why he found Phillipe's suggestion, on the face of it, completely incomprehensible. What if she didn't want to stay? Of course she would stay. She *had* to stay, because... because he wanted her to.

Gabriel was a profound egoist; no one could have endured what he had without becoming one in mere self-defense. But even he recognized the flaw in that logic. Gillian had accused him of treating her like a favorite pet, and he had been amused. He did not like to think there might be some truth in her observation.

He stood and began to pace the width of the small chamber. Today he was wearing the short leather breeches and open robe in which he was most comfortable, and as he moved the robe fluttered out behind him, reminding him of the tactile sensation of a soft wind catching a sail. Once he had sailed. Once he had done many things. All of them had lost their appeal for him ... until Gillian.

But she was no ordinary woman. She was smart, capable, inquisitive, tenacious, inventive, resourceful, independent—and those were only a few of the things he found fascinating about her. Her adoration was not guaranteed; she could not be manipulated or commanded or persuaded into compliancy. For all those reasons, she was exciting—and dangerous.

What if she did not want to stay?

He tried to imagine a time when he would grow tired of her, as he had done with so many things over the years. It was impossible to do, and just how impossible it was startled him. She had brought so many things into his life, and he had not begun to explore them all. The absurdities and the mysteries of the outside world, her own brash impertinence, wonder and youthful impatience and curiosity...

Ah yes, wonder. That was what she had brought to him that was of the most significance. That was invaluable, irreplaceable, that he could not imagine having lived without for so long. Wonder. How could he give it up now, having barely tasted it?

Gabriel had sacrificed a great many things in his lifetime; he had stood by and watched, unprotesting, as all that he valued disappeared. But this one thing... He was not ready to let her go. Not yet.

What if she did not want to stay?

She would. Because he wanted her to, and the alternative was unthinkable.

GILLIAN WAS FASCINATED by the children of this place, and she spent a good part of her free time in the play area, watching them. With children, language was no barrier, and they seemed to find her just as delightful as she did them.

Sometimes she persuaded Gabriel to accompany her on her playroom visits, though always through his impatient protests. "You really are a horrible grouch," she told him. "The stereotypical bachelor."

"I'm not at all sure what you intend by that, but I don't think I like it."

They had left the playroom, with its noisy, enthusiastic collection of toddlers and preschoolers, and wandered into an adjacent chamber which was reminiscent of an amphitheater. Stone benches encircled the walls two stories high, and in the center a group of older children appeared to be enacting some kind of drama. Gillian wished she understood the language, for Gabriel looked far too bored to interpret for her.

"Everyone likes children," she insisted.

"They are bothersome and noisy and impossible to hold an intelligent conversation with," he replied shortly. "Are you certain you can't think of anything more interesting to do?"

At that moment a young girl saw Gillian and broke from the group, running toward them with a broad welcoming smile. An older woman, apparently the children's supervisor, called after her, but she ignored her. The girl caught Gillian's hand, and Gillian bent down to greet her, returning the smile.

The girl burst forth with something in the sweet musical language of hers, and impulsively she reached for Gabriel's hand as well, seeming to want to urge them inside. But Gabriel took an abrupt step back and spoke to the girl shortly in her own language. The child dropped her eyes and returned quickly to the group.

Gillian stared at Gabriel. "That was rude," she said with some surprise.

He frowned a little. "I merely told her her teacher was calling."

"You hurt her feelings."

"That's absurd."

His tone was far too brusque for Gillian's liking, and it nettled her. "Well, at least I know one thing about you now, as mysterious as you'd like to keep yourself. You've obviously never had any children—nor are you likely to, with that attitude.''

Something flashed in his eyes that took Gillian completely by surprise, a powerful mix of emotion that left her unable, for that moment, to even interpret what she saw there. Was it hurt, anger... or protest?

He said coldly, "*That* was rude."

He turned away, and Gillian thought he would walk off and leave her there. Perhaps that was his intention, but after a moment she saw the tension in his shoulders forcefully relax, and he turned back to her. The anger in his eyes was gone, leaving a weary apology. His voice was gentler.

"I have no wish to argue with you over such a foolish matter," he said, offering his hand. "If you like, we will go inside and watch the children."

Gillian hesitated. What she wanted to do was find out exactly what had brought that awful look to his eyes, and what it meant, but she knew that to pursue that line of questioning would only push him farther away from her. She knew, as well, that he had no desire to watch the play the children were performing, but she would be foolish to reject his overture of peace.

She glanced inside uncertainly. "I don't want to interrupt them."

"The acoustics are carefully designed. We can sit at the top and talk, and they will never know we're here."

Gillian followed him up the stone steps to the top bleacher. Today he was wearing khaki trousers and a field jacket whose design might have been copied from some long-ago jungle explorer. His long hair was pulled back and tied at the nape and, except for thong sandals, his feet were bare. His costumes—for Gillian always thought of them as such—seemed designed to amuse her, but he wore all of them so effortlessly and so well that the image he portrayed was never anything less than one of authority—and sexiness.

She sat beside him at the top of the stadium, her attention divided between the players on the stage below and the man who sat beside her. Of the two, she found Gabriel by far the more interesting, and she had to force herself to concentrate on the children.

"They are rehearsing for a pageant," Gabriel told her. "It's a reenactment of a creation legend, and really quite fascinating."

Gillian smiled. "I'm glad to hear you think so."

"I'm merely trying not to be a grouch," he replied.

Their eyes met then with a smile and held in a way that made Gillian's heart catch. It was impossible to remain annoyed with him for long. Impossible to be anything except eternally fascinated by him, eternally delighted. . . .

She turned her attention quickly back to the stage.

Although she couldn't understand the language, Gillian found it surprisingly easy to follow the play, for the theme was universal and children were children everywhere. In addition, there was something very westernized about the players' movements and gestures, making the little drama seem more like the school pageant Gabriel had described than the tribal ritual Gillian might have expected. And that was not the only evidence of European influence Gillian had noticed as she wandered through the complex, and now saw repeated on the stage before her. Although most of the children possessed the nut-brown skin and blunt features she had come to identify the natives of this place, many of them showed other ancestry in their lighter skin and more delicate bone structure. Gillian wondered how many generations ago this pure Indian race had begun intermarrying with outsiders, and how it had begun.

And, remembering his earlier peculiar behavior—and despite her accusations—Gillian couldn't help wondering if any of the children were Gabriel's.

She glanced at him and was ashamed to find herself examining his face for some sign of paternal pride or particular affection. All she saw was a mild, mostly impersonal boredom.

At that moment a squabble that apparently wasn't in the script broke out onstage among two older boys, and a woman came rushing forward to intervene, scolding them loudly. Gillian smiled. Constantly she was being reminded by incidents such as these that, no matter how out of the ordinary—even bizarre—life in this place might seem at times, it was in fact very real.

"Do they go to school with organized classrooms like children in other countries do?" Gillian asked.

"I really don't know," Gabriel replied, and gestured her to precede him down the stairs. "Shall we go? I don't often take an interest in the day-to-day lives of these people," he added by way of explanation.

"That's odd." Gillian started down the stairs.

"Is it?"

"Well, yes. I mean, you're obviously the most advantaged party here—better educated, more well traveled, with greater resources—it would seem inevitable for the missionary syndrome to kick in. You know, that you would feel paternal—" *There's that word again,* she thought "—toward the lesser culture and educate them to your standards. Or, at least, feel superior while trying."

"It's not my place."

"Must take a pretty noble character to resist the temptation."

"Not really."

His voice was flat, and when she glanced over her shoulder she found a mask had come over his features that was chill and remote. She saw she had touched a nerve but couldn't imagine how—or why.

Sensing her puzzlement, he gave her a smile that was designed to put her at ease but never reached his eyes. "You'll find, my dear Miss Gillian Aldair—although I suppose I should be calling you Doctor, shouldn't I?—that nobility is not one of my vices. It's dreadfully dull and requires far too much effort on my part."

He touched her back lightly as they reached the bottom of the stairs, guiding her toward the door. "As for how these people may or may not run their lives, I'm sure my presence among them has influenced their culture in certain ways, but I hardly keep a catalog of those ways. I simply don't have the interest."

Gillian suspected there was a great deal more to the story than that, but chose not to pursue it at this point.

As they passed the playroom again, she noticed for the first time the oddly shaped block of wood that was being used as a doorstop. She knelt down to examine it closer, and caught her breath.

"Gabriel . . . do you know what this is?"

"Hmm. Part of a lintel, I believe. I think it once decorated a temple of sorts."

Gillian's heart was beating hard and fast. "There's writing here!" In fact, the lintel was covered with writing—pictographs in a language she had never seen before.

"Take it back to your room, if you like," he offered. "Study it."

She stared at him. "This could be thousands of years old!"

"Eight thousand, six hundred forty-three, by my calculations."

She continued to stare at him, shocked into near motionlessness by his easy confidence. But when he extended a casual hand to help her to her feet, she quickly snatched up the artifact and stood. "That's impossible."

He shrugged and dropped his hand. They resumed walking. "There's no evidence whatsoever to indicate there was ever a civilization of any sort in these mountains that long ago," she insisted.

"After eight thousand years there wouldn't be, would there?"

"How can you know?" she demanded, much against her better judgment. "How can you possibly know?"

He just smiled.

She shook her head again.

"Impossible. How would they live in this climate, anyway? The land isn't arable, there's precious little water, and, for that matter, where did the trees come from?" She shook the lintel at him. "For this...."

"But the landscape was quite different eight thousand years ago," he assured her. "Once the land was lush and rich with volcanic ash, terraced for agriculture...." And then he glanced at her indulgently. "But I am spoiling your fun. Find out for yourself."

Gillian studied the carvings, wondering if what he said was possible, wondering if the writings held the clue, and feeling the old frustration of confronting a mystery she could not solve. "If I had my notes," she muttered, "I'll bet I could make a good start on interpreting this."

"Shall I read it for you?" he offered casually.

She scowled at him. "Now you've gone too far. No one on earth can read this. It's in no known language. I'm an expert on languages and I can't read it. What makes you think you can just pick it up and read it like a book?"

"Actually," he replied, "it isn't that obscure. If you'll notice the root language is the same as that used by the Maya and certain tribes of the American Plains—" Noting her expression, he broke off and smiled apologetically. "I am spoiling your fun again."

"The Maya *have* no root language in common with the American Indians."

His expression remained bland. "I see."

"And even if they did, the Mayan language hasn't been completely broken yet."

He seemed surprised by this. "Oh."

"Why do you say such outrageous things?"

That amused him. "They only seem outrageous to you. You should hear how the things you say sound to *me*."

Gillian opened her mouth to retort, but then she had to know. "What does it say?" she demanded, indicating the artifact.

His eyes twinkled mildly. "'Abandon all hope, ye who enter here.'"

"You are impossible!" She lengthened her stride, scowling at the scrap of wood in her hand. "Just when I almost think I should take you seriously—"

"Always take me seriously, dear heart. I forgot how to joke before you were born."

Once again she drew a breath, but let her reply die unspoken. "I don't know why I bother arguing with you, anyway," she grumbled, returning her gaze to the artifact. "I don't even know where we are, or where you found this, or that you didn't make it yourself with a pen knife, or even steal it from our camp."

He looked hurt. Gillian could not be sure how much of the expression was feigned.

"I do not traffic in frauds, I assure you. I hardly have any need for that."

Given what she had seen so far, Gillian had to agree with him there.

"And I certainly didn't go to all the trouble of stealing a scrap of doorframe from your camp—when I have dozens of such things lying about which are of no use to me—only to give it back to you as a gift. And I have told you where we are—deep inside what you call the Andes mountains of South America, some ten miles from your original camp. In less than one breath you've accused me of lying, cheating and stealing, and you hardly know me well enough to assign me any kind of label. I wonder what I must do to earn your trust."

Though his tone was mild and his expression bland, the truth was inflammatory enough, and equally undeniable. Gillian felt instantly uncomfortable. "You're the one who said nobility wasn't one of your vices."

He shot her an amused glance. "So I did."

Gillian was relieved to see the smile in his eyes, and she relaxed. But she had to ask, "Does it really matter to you whether I trust you?"

His expression grew thoughtful, and for one of the few times since she had known him, Gillian was certain he was being absolutely sincere. He answered in a tone that sounded a little surprised. "Oddly enough, it does." He looked at her for a moment and puzzlement faintly shadowed his crystal-blue eyes. Then he smiled and touched her arm lightly. "I can't think why. Come this way. I want to show you something truly spectacular."

They walked down the main corridor again, with Gillian unable to resist the temptation to tilt her head back constantly to admire the play of light on the breezy gauze ceiling. She repeatedly noticed one picturesque aspect to the atmosphere that nonetheless seemed somehow out of place: stern-featured young men in short, white toga-like costumes, with sheathed daggers at their sides. They seemed out of place because theirs were the first weapons Gillian had ever seen here.

When she asked Gabriel about them, his reply was perfunctory. "They're called Protectors. Their function is purely decorative now, but in ancient times I believe they were an elite few selected to guard this place against intruders—and to prevent others from leaving, if memory serves."

Gillian would have liked to have pursued that, but Gabriel dismissed the subject. He guided her toward a left fork and away from the main boulevard; the walls once again became plain stone, the ceiling distant and dim.

"How big is this place, anyway?" she asked.

He was thoughtful. "In truth, I'm not really sure. So much of it is unused. There's a map somewhere, I think."

"And you don't have any idea who built it, or how or why?"

He drew a breath to reply, but she interrupted sternly. "And don't start trying to sell me that line about how you tunneled it all out yourself with earth movers and dynamite just so you'd have a summer hideaway. I'm almost ready to believe you might have wired the living quarters for electricity—though how, I still can't figure out—but that is absolutely as far as I'm willing to go."

A tightening of his lips repressed a smile. "Perhaps it all is the work of your ancient lost tribe."

After a moment, one corner of Gillian's lips turned downward with a dry smile. "Perhaps."

The corridor, though still magically lit by that source she had not yet been able to identify, was beginning to take on a slightly musty, earthen odor that indicated it was seldom used. The echo of their footsteps reminded Gillian that they were, in fact, walking through a tunnel. She should perhaps have felt uneasy in this strange place alone with this inarguably strange man—but in fact she had never felt safer in her life.

She glanced at him, strong and commanding as he walked beside her. So many times when she looked at him, images of military or imperial leaders came to mind—general, prince, king, commander—and she decided now that it must be because of his bearing, the way he held his head and shoulders, the way he walked. He was no ordinary man, and that was evident in every inch of him. She only wished she knew what *kind* of man, exactly, he was.

"How did you find out about the landslide, anyway?" she asked. "How did you know I was trapped?"

He hesitated, then glanced at her. "You are familiar with the telescope?"

"Of course."

He seemed a little relieved to discover that, which Gillian would have found amusing if it had not been so bizarre. "I have a similar device," he said. "It's designed to register changes in the natural environment and can be made to focus much like a telescope."

Gillian frowned. "I never heard of anything like that."

"Look."

He stopped at the curved, roughly hewn doorway of a chamber and gestured her inside, smiling. Gillian stepped over the threshold and caught her breath.

"Oh my..."

Gabriel came to stand beside her. "I told you it was spectacular."

They were standing inside a natural geode. The largest one Gillian had ever seen was in a museum of natural history, a quartz-crystal geode that measured roughly six by two feet. The hollow stone in which they now stood was ten by twelve by ten feet high, and it was lined, ceiling and walls, with crystal-pointed, gem-quality amethyst.

Light twinkled and sparked off a hundred thousand points of rich grape jewel, shades of purple from lavender to violet and every nuance in between were reflected in an endless glassy kaleidoscope of winking lights and dizzying colors. Beyond her first breathless exclamation, Gillian could not think of a single thing to say. It was enough to simply stand there and look around and be entranced.

"When I was a younger man I used to come here often," he said. "It was considered quite the spot for young lovers then, but now I think it's mostly been forgotten. A pity," he mused. "Even in this unspoiled place, romance will eventually give way to mundanity."

"I don't understand," Gillian said with difficulty, "how anyone could ever forget a place like *this*." Her eyes practically ached with the beauty of the room. She had to deliberately look away, focusing on Gabriel. "This is more than romantic. It's—" She gestured expansively, searching for words. "It's magical."

"Ah, yes," he said softly, watching her. "Once I believed in magic. Just as once I believed in love."

Gillian looked up at him, her heart beating tightly in her chest. "And now you don't?"

He lifted a hand and touched her hair. Light danced and sparkled all around them, on his skin, in his eyes, in the air between them. He said huskily, "I've lived too long and seen too much. There's little left for me to believe in. And yet, I sometimes think..." His hand drifted down to her shoulder, his eyes following the curve of her neck and her arm. "If you asked me to, Gillian Aldair, I could believe in almost anything."

*Words,* she thought, a little dizzily, *only words....* Yet when he said them, their seductive power was intense, their meaning real. "We have a lot in common," she answered, barely above a whisper.

A shadowy smile touched his features, though perhaps it was only the light. "Because you don't believe in love, either."

"Because," she said, reaching up to grasp his finger, "you could make me believe in anything, too. Almost."

And then she had to look away. She removed his fingers from her shoulder and took a deep breath, forcing a smile as she looked around.

"Anyway," she murmured, "how could you not belive in magic in a place like this? It's otherworldly. Celestial. Almost...hallowed. What is that quote about the meeting place between the mortal and the divine? It's like that."

He smiled. "Socrates is credited with saying that love is the intermediary between the mortal and the divine, if that's the quote you refer to."

"Yes, that's it." Once again her eyes were drawn around the room in pure sensual appreciation. She felt bathed in light, awash in color, tingling with rich purple warmth.

"He didn't say it, of course."

"Who?"

"Socrates."

Gillian returned her gaze to him. She couldn't help observing that this background was perfectly suited to Gabriel. Purple, the color of royalty. Amethyst, the symbol of wealth. "He didn't?"

"Of course not. He couldn't possibly have said one half of what is credited to him."

Her curiosity was beginning to turn to skepticism. "Then who did?"

A mild twinkle graced his eyes as he glanced down at her. "Some obscure student now long forgotten."

"Hmm." She linked her hands behind her, gazing up at the jeweled ceiling again. "And now I suppose you'll tell me Shakespeare didn't write his poems, either."

"Certainly he did. It was the plays he was prone to borrow."

Gillian laughed, turning to him. The sound of her laughter seemed to play off the jeweled walls and be caught up in the light, reflected finally in his eyes. "You really are outrageous. Is that all you do—sit here day after day and formulate wild unprovable theories?"

"In part." Though his tone was easy, his eyes moved over her, filled with the electric energy, and there was a quickening of awareness between them. The jeweled chamber was small and they stood close; magic seemed at that moment only a heartbeat away.

"And the other parts?"

A movement pulsed in expectation as his eyes rested upon her mouth. He had been nothing but the gentleman since the moment he had given her his promise, and now was apparently not the time he intended to change his mind—or perhaps he just meant to torment her. He glanced away, breaking the spell and replied casually, "I have my hobbies."

From somewhere within the room she heard the swell of music, so clear and so near that she actually turned full circle, searching overhead for a balcony and within the walls for an opening. "Is that an orchestra?"

"No. A reproduction." He hesitated. "Are you familiar with such things?"

"Do you mean like a CD?"

A small frown appeared on his brow. "That would stand for—?"

She made no effort to disguise her skepticism. "Compact disc. You can operate a high-tech telescope that can focus in on an injured person beneath a ton of earth ten miles away but you've never heard of a compact disc?"

He merely shrugged. "Perhaps I simply know it by a different name."

"If so, you should get into the business. I've never heard a compact disc sound this good. Never."

The tune was compelling, poignant but soothing. It had none of the electronic overtones that marked so many modern compositions, yet it had a definite New Age feel. She listened for a while, enraptured by the music, the magical room...and him.

"It's beautiful," she said softly.

"Thank you. One of my hobbies."

She turned to look at him. "You composed that?"

He nodded.

Gillian's eyes moved over him slowly, absorbing, memorizing, assuring herself that the man she saw before her wouldn't evaporate with the next breath. "Sometimes," she said, "I don't think you can be real."

His expression was sober, his eyes shadowed. "I am real, Gillian," he said quietly. "Though I sometimes wish it were not so, I am very, very real."

Then abruptly he turned away. With a lift of his hand the music stopped and he gestured her toward the door. "But I grow bored talking about myself. Tell me of Gillian, and her world."

She had no choice but to follow his change of mood. "My world is very ordinary," she told him. With reluctance she followed him out of the magical little chamber and back into the corridor.

"Not to me," he assured her.

"After all this—" she made a helpless gesture that was meant to indicate everything she had seen so far "—I would hardly know what to say. I mean, what could possibly interest you about where I come from?"

"Everything," he replied promptly. "What your home is like, what your work is like, what you do for recreation, what your newspapers say. What you find fascinating, what you find mundane, what you have learned in the past year that amazes you the most—"

"You," she interrupted without qualification. "I've learned about you—not nearly enough, it's true, but I intend to learn a great deal more—and that will amaze me for the rest of my life."

He smiled. It was the kind of smile that had a hint of surprise to it, which Gillian found very gratifying. She had a feeling he was not a man who was surprised often, and that look in his eyes made him seem more human, somehow.

"I am serious, Gillian," he said.

"And you think I'm not?"

"Tell me, for example," he insisted, "what we would be doing now if I were your beau."

She felt the brush of his fire-blue gaze tingling along her skin, teasing her, coaxing. It was all she could do to keep from blushing.

"You're not my beau."

"Pretend."

They had once again reached the airy light-filled main corridor. There were sounds of distant activity and occasionally someone passed, nodded and smiled on the opposite side of the passage. The sense of intimacy should have dissipated, but, in fact, it only increased in this romantic setting of moving light and soft shadows. Or perhaps it was simply that—as she was rapidly discovering—anywhere she was with this man was romantic.

"That's a very old-fashioned word," she said.

"Shall I choose another?"

She glanced up at him and was struck, in a mostly pleasant way, by how appropriately that phrase described him. Old-fashioned, with all its connotations of elegance and gracious living and order. "No," she said, and now she did feel the faintest tingle of a blush warm her cheeks. "I kind of like it."

He reached for her hand and tucked it protectively through his arm as they walked, another courtly, old-fashioned gesture that was performed almost as though on cue. "Then tell me."

Gillian smiled to herself, thinking for a moment before she answered. "All right. If you were my boyfriend—beau—we probably would have met at school, which would mean we've had lunch together a few times already with a couple of other staff members, or maybe just shared a sandwich on a bench outside the library...."

He smiled, as though enjoying that image.

"Then one day you would have called me up—"

"As on the telephone?"

She shot him an amused glance. "Yes. On the telephone. And you would have asked me to dinner and a movie."

He frowned a little. "This would be a moving-picture show?"

She chuckled. "You have had an erratic education, haven't you. Of course, trying to impress me, you would have suggested Chez Robert—that's the fanciest restaurant in town, which means they use cloth napkins—and the Twelfth Street Theater, which is always playing foreign-film festivals. I, on the other hand, would much prefer pizza and anything starring Kevin Costner, and because I hardly ever get to go out, I probably would have wheedled you into doing what I wanted. And we both would have a lot more fun than if we'd gone with your plan."

He looked thoroughly puzzled by the entire re-
cital, but all he said was, "What is pizza?"

She laughed, briefly squeezing his arm in affection as she did. "You *would* be a fun date!"

He smiled, her laughter reflected in the sparks of
his eyes. "And then what would we do? After the
pizza and the moving pictures?"

"Oh, I don't know." Her expression grew
thoughtful as she tried to take herself back there, to
a place so far removed in space and time it might
have been on another planet... and yet, now that he
had reminded her of it, suddenly, painfully close.
"We might go for a drive out to Pearson's Cove and
watch the moon on the water or, maybe, if the night
was warm, take off our shoes and go wading.... Or
maybe you'd just walk me home and we'd sit on the
porch and talk. Or have a hot-fudge sundae at the Ice
Cream Palace, if it wasn't too late. People still do
that kind of corny stuff where I come from, which is
one reason I've always liked living there so much."

Her voice took on a dreamy, reminiscent quality,
and for a moment she really was back there, bringing it all to life for this exotic stranger. "It's such a
perfect town, like something out of an old Jimmy
Stewart movie. There really is an Elm Street, and it
really is lined with huge old elm trees. All the street
lamps have funny, old-fashioned globes and all the
houses have big front porches. And people walk
home from the movies at night without getting

mugged, and sit on the front porches in big wicker chairs and watch the stars. It's...nice. Really nice."

He stopped and, taking her lightly by the shoulders, turned her to face him. "And when we reached that big front porch of yours," he said softly, "what would happen then? Would we share a kiss that tasted of summertime? Would we tell secrets and make promises meant to last a lifetime? Would we fall in love beneath the big silver moon of your sleepy little town?"

Gillian was mesmerized by his eyes, his husky, sensuous voice, the touch of his fingers on her arms. She could feel her heartbeat skipping in her chest and blood tingling with expectation in her veins. "Falling in love," she whispered, "is meant for magical places like this."

He lifted a hand to smooth back her hair, and his eyes followed the movement, lightening and darkening over the planes of her face. "You excite me, Gillian," he said. "You make me think, you make me feel, you make me glad to be awake each day. You have brought magic back into this place, and you almost make me believe in it. Yet...when you talk of the world you left behind, there's sadness in your eyes, and I don't want to think I put the sadness there. Do you miss it, Gillian?" he asked quietly. "Have I made you homesick?"

"In a way," she admitted, considering her answer. "But in a way—no. You make me remember the good things, but before I came here...I was so tired. Life was black-and-white. Nothing excited me, nothing challenged me, nothing even interested me very much."

Her voice dropped a fraction, and she put her thoughts into words more for herself than for him. "When I was hurt—when I was lying there before you came, paralyzed and helpless and in so much pain—I thought about how easy it would be to just give up. But now I'm glad I didn't."

She lifted her eyes to him. "I came on the expedition looking for more than a lost tribe, you know. I was looking for a way to feel alive again. And now..." Her lips tightened with a small smile. "I'll tell you a secret. Even though I know I can't stay, that I only found this place by accident in the most literal sense of the word, sometimes it seems the life I've known here seems more real than the one I left behind.

"I'm still not sure about all this...." She made a small indicative gesture with her wrist. "It still scares me in some ways. I'm still not sure about you, and you make me crazy with all your contradictions and mysteries—but I wouldn't have missed this for the world," she told him sincerely. "No matter what happens, no matter what comes of this, my life will never be the same for having met you, Gabriel. And I'll never be sorry for that."

His hands cupped her face lightly, fingertips spreading over her temples. Warmth and strength surrounded her, and in his eyes she saw forever. He said gently, "That's all anyone can ask, isn't it? To have at least one thing in life he doesn't regret."

Then he leaned forward and kissed her tenderly on the forehead. "I hope," he said softly, "that I can say the same of you when the time comes for us to part."

## Chapter Six

Gillian and Gabriel were sharing a meal in a sun-speckled glade fed by the same stream that meandered through the agricultural area. She had wanted to see if the grass was real. It was. So was the water, though Gabriel did confess its color had been enhanced by specially treated stones lining the streambed.

Just like an amusement park.

Today Gillian wore a pale green embroidered shirt with an ankle-length divided skirt of darker green. One of the young girls had braided her hair with a sprig of sweet-smelling flower entwined in its locks. Since she had complained to him about it, Gillian's wardrobe had been supplemented with a variety of costumes—and costumes they were, ranging from the elegant bare-shouldered Grecian gown to glittering satin evening wear to velveteen riding habits. Nowhere was there a pair of jeans or a sweater, and Gillian found it impossible to make the women understand what she meant when she described them. So she made do with what she found—colorful skirts that stopped just above her ankles, pretty leg-of-mutton blouses, romantic Empire-waisted gowns and fringed shawls that she used to belt loose-fitting shifts. Choosing her clothing for the day was something to which she had never before given the slightest moment's thought; now it became an essential part of the fun.

She tilted her head back, trying to detect the elaborate network of mirrors that Gabriel insisted was responsible for the gently filtered sunlight that flooded the interior. What she saw overhead was an illusion of sky and fluffy white clouds gently moving with the spin of the planet.

"Amazing," she murmured. "You really do have everything you need here. I mean, a person might get tired of looking at incredible works of art or reading rare books or lying around on silk sofas or bathing in mineral springs…he might want to walk in a park now and then. So why not just make one?"

He stretched out beside her on the grass, smiling at her, his head propped up on one elbow. His hair was tied back at the nape, his open-throated white shirt was belted like a tunic over tight-fitting dark breeches. He might have been any ordinary man enjoying a picnic with any ordinary woman in any ordinary place in the world. But he wasn't, and she wasn't, and this wasn't.

"You look lovely today," he said.

A little self-consciously, she fussed with the flowers in her hair. "I feel like a wood nymph. Not exactly my style."

"Oh, I don't know. I think you might have made a perfectly acceptable wood nymph."

She leaned back on her elbows, crossing her legs at the ankles as she stretched out on the grass. The movement brought her close to him, and it was comfortable. "Look. Is that a catwalk up there? Does it go all the way to the top?"

"Hmm. It's part of the scaffolding the workmen used. Toward the top it gives way to iron handholds fastened into the rock. And that's not really the top, you know—just an air shaft."

She glanced at him. "How far underground *are* we?"

His smile deepened, as it always did when he found her questions amusing or precocious—a clear signal he did not intend to answer. "Significantly."

She dismissed it, turning her face back to the warmth of the sun—artificially enhanced though it might be. "Is this how you keep your tan? By coming here?"

"I don't have a tan." She looked at him, ready to argue, and he explained, "This is my natural skin pigment. I am of Mediterranean descent."

That was the first thing of an even remotely personal nature he had ever said to her, and she wanted to pursue it. But he distracted her by holding up his hand as though to compare skin colors; she lowered herself to one elbow and held her hand up beside his.

His hand was large and golden brown; hers was small and, even with the fading tan she had acquired while working at the dig, pale in comparison. Gabriel turned his hand over and slid it beneath hers, palm to palm. The contact quickened her pulse, ever so slightly.

Deliberately bringing her thoughts back on course, she said, "So that's your accent. Greek?"

"It might be." A sparkle in his eyes revealed that he recognized her attempt to, once again, pump him for information. "I speak many languages, you know."

"But that's not your nationality?"

He entwined his fingers with hers, an enchantingly sweet, old-fashioned gesture. "Not exactly."

She had to concentrate to maintain her determination, for the warm strength of his hand around hers, the slight caressing movement he made with his thumb over the pulse point of her wrist, was a strong temptation to relax and let him lead the way. She firmly decided on a frontal assault. "Where, then? Where were you born?"

He merely smiled, lowering his eyes to their entwined hands. "It was a small country, which, due to a series of political upheavals, is no longer in existence. So you see, I'm afraid I am a man of no nationality."

She sighed, giving in with a shake of her head. "Do you know, I sometimes think this mystery-man persona of yours is not such a bad idea. You're a lot more fun to fantasize about than I'm sure you would be in the dull harsh light of the truth."

He chuckled. She loved the way his eyes gave off azure sparks when he did so.

"Is that a fact?"

"Oh, yes. In my fantasies, you are an exiled prince, a revolutionary in hiding, an eccentric millionaire, a mad genius, a rock star.... In reality, you're probably just crazy."

Again he laughed. "And what if I were to tell you I am all those things?" And he paused thoughtfully. "Except the rock star. I'm almost certain I'm not that."

She turned on her elbow to face him. "Including crazy?"

"Definitely crazy." He brought their entwined hands to her face and lightly caressed the shape of her chin with his index finger. "Since I met you, more than ever."

Gillian looked at him for another moment, wondering not who he was or where he was from or how shy he was here, but how it would feel to touch the smooth arch of his cheekbone, to spread her fingers through his hair.

"I think I would believe you," she said. She shifted her weight again, turning to look back at the sky. Her fingers remained entwined with his. "And that would be the first thing I've believed since I got here."

With two fingers he caressed the circlet of her wedding ring. "Why do you wear this? You told me your husband was dead."

That was not a subject she had expected him to raise. A shivery little note of reality had suddenly been injected into the fairy-tale-perfect atmosphere, and she slowly pulled her hand away.

"He is," she answered quietly. "It was a lingering illness and very painful—for both of us. Cancer. I don't like to talk about it."

"Cancer," he repeated, looking mildly interested. "They still treat that with radioactive materials, don't they?"

She looked at him sharply. "That's an odd thing for a doctor to say. Of course they do."

"Barbaric," he muttered.

Gillian's heart began to pound, as it always did when he said something or did something that was just a little off-key like that, not easy to dissect but not quite right, either. Her voice was a little more strident than the circumstances dictated as she demanded, "You have a more effective therapy?"

He looked for a moment as though he might answer, then said instead, "I asked why you wear the ring."

Gillian forced her muscles to relax, forced her mind to let go of the idea that was disturbing her much in the same way she would unclench her fist to release a weapon. She should have pursued it. Even then she knew she should have. But even then she also knew there were some questions to which she didn't really want to know the answers.

"I wear it to honor his memory," she replied. She brought her ring hand to her chest as though to protect it. "Because I mourn him, and miss him."

"And so you can be sad every time you look at it."

She cast a sharp glance at him, but his expression surprised her. It was brooding and troubled, his gaze fixed on the slim gold band on her finger.

"Don't be sorry for him," he said briefly. "His troubles are over. Be glad for him, if anything. He's the lucky one."

It was a surprising sentiment to hear expressed by him, and for a moment she didn't know how to reply.

"That may be," she answered carefully, "but I still miss him. I never counted on losing him so soon and . . . I'm sorry."

He turned a thoughtful, skeptical look on her. "You wanted him to live forever?"

She was glimpsing a cruel streak in him that didn't so much surprise her as puzzle her, for she didn't think he meant to be cruel. She swallowed hard. "Yes. Of course. You always want the ones you love to live forever."

He gave a short, harsh laugh. "What fools you are." He sat up, resting one arm across an upraised knee as he looked at her. There was impatience in his eyes and a kind of hardness she did not like. "You needn't hide your hand as though you're afraid I'll steal the ring right off your finger. I've told you before, I won't take anything you're not willing to give."

She tilted her chin and replied coolly, "That's very generous of you, I'm sure."

The position of the sun had not changed, nor had the clouds grown thicker, but the glade in which they sat seemed a little dimmer now, a little cooler. Gillian hated that. A moment ago everything had been so glorious.

As though reading her thoughts, he said brusquely, "This is absurdity, to spend such a day talking about another man. Let us turn to pleasanter subjects."

She wasn't quite ready to let him off the hook that easily. "Such as yourself?"

The tension left the lines around his mouth with his smile. "I said pleasant. Such as you, Gillian Aldair. What is your style?"

That was sufficiently distracting to make her forget she was supposed to be cross with him. "What?"

"Earlier you said your style was not that of the wood nymph. Because I am eager to see you live your life in grand high style, I would like to know what that style is."

Almost against her will, a soft laugh escaped her. He was the most incorrigible man. Infuriating, intimidating, incomprehensible and even a little frightening sometimes . . . but always irresistible.

"I'm not sure I know the answer to that," she admitted. "Maybe I used to, but now I'm not so sure."

"Is this a bad thing?"

She shrugged, a little uncomfortable. She had never been very good at self-examination, and she certainly hadn't expected the conversation to take such a philosophical turn.

"I don't know the answer to that, either. My father used to say everybody needs to be shaken up every once in a while, just to put things in perspective." She paused a moment, thinking about that.

"He sounds like a wise man."

"He is," she agreed musingly. "I don't think I appreciated that particular piece of wisdom enough until recently, though." Again she shrugged, threading her fingers through the fine thick carpet of grass. "I don't know. I think my style is—was—kind of intent and humorless. Ambitious. Determined. Fixed on one straight path with no detours."

"Except for the one you took to get here," he pointed out.

She cast him a wry look. "Exactly. I guess I should add impatience to that list, and I always knew it was the kind of impatience that would get me in trouble one day. That's not exactly a good characteristic for a scientist, anyway, you know. It can lead to short-cuts."

She had never admitted that to anyone before; she wasn't even sure she had fully recognized it herself until now. It bothered her, but not as much as it should have.

"Anyway," she concluded, "I've always thought of my style as being distinctly straightforward and unimaginative. There's never been anything glamorous or fanciful about me. And all this..." She lifted her hand and waved it through the air. "*This* is not my style. I shouldn't even be here, much less actually enjoying it."

He lifted his hand, winding a tendril of her hair around his index finger. His smile made her feel beautiful, feminine, fanciful and romantic...all the things she had never been.

"I'm glad you're enjoying it, Gillian. I sometimes think I created it just for you."

Instinctively she turned her cheek into his caress. *This isn't my style, either... listening to romantic nonsense from an enigmatic stranger who could be anything from a mad scientist to a mass murderer. And liking it. Even half believing it.*

It was with an effort that she anchored herself to reality again, focusing on the silver band he wore on the middle finger of his left hand. She had noticed it before but never considered its significance until today.

"You wear a ring," she pointed out. "Are you married?"

"It's not a wedding band."

His hand left her cheek and he held out his fingers to better display the ring. It was not worn on the traditional ring finger, nor did it resemble a traditional wedding band. It was inscribed around with drawings that were too fine for Gillian to read, and it had a heavy, antique look to it.

"It's a magic ring," he told her. "Customarily worn by sorcerers in the Middle Ages."

Gillian took his fingers in hers, examining the ring more closely. Her heart sped a little, though she could not be certain whether it was from excitement over the purported antiquity of the ring, or the intimacy that brought their heads close together, their fingers in warm contact.

She looked up at him. His face was close enough to brush with her cheek; his eyes seemed to have replaced the sky.

"Are you a sorcerer?" she asked, a little huskily.

He smiled. "I might be . . . if these were the Middle Ages."

Gillian was unable to take her gaze from his. She didn't want to. "I think you would be in any century," she said softly. "I think you are now."

He slipped his hand behind her neck. Gillian's heart beat wild and fast as he lowered his face to hers, dark blue eyes burning flaming heat through her as they neared. His mouth covered hers.

It was like being caught in a fast-moving stream, tumbling, swirling, rushing. She lost herself in colors and heat, in the explosion of chemical awareness, in his strength, in his power. He drank her in and she was eager to be absorbed. He overwhelmed her and she joyously surrendered. Her muscles trembled, her heartbeat shook her chest, dizziness roared in her head. Never had she been kissed like that. Never had she known a man like this.

"Now tell me, beloved." His voice was low and hot in her ear, reverberating through her blood. "Was that so dread a thing? So worthy of all your protests?"

His hands encircled her upper arms, his lips pressed heated kisses deep into the curve of her neck. His strength went through her and robbed her of her own; each clasp of his lips upon her skin sent a new rush of dizziness through her.

"You taste like jasmine," he murmured.

"Stop," she whispered, struggling to regain her breath. "This isn't— I can't think—"

"You're not supposed to think." He gathered her close to him again, pressing her into the hardness of his muscled chest, and his kiss was strong and demanding, fiercely possessive. "I don't want you to think." He flooded her face with his breath, his taste, his solid strong invasive presence. "I want your head to spin. I want you to feel things you've never felt before, Gillian, and I can make that happen for you. From now on when you fantasize about me, dream on this. . . ."

This time when he covered her parted lips with his own, it was an invasion, certain and thorough and powerful, flooding her senses and filling her veins and robbing her of reason and will and the need for either. His tongue claimed hers in a fierce abandoned mating dance, and sharp arrows of need stabbed from the pulse of her throat to the core of her womb. Her arms encircled his neck and she clung to him, fingers tangling in the silk of his hair. His hands were hard against the side of her face, worshiping her, demanding her, conquering and wooing and leaving her helpless with desire. Dream of him? Would she ever dream of anything else?

"Have you any thoughts left?" he demanded huskily against her open mouth. His breath, heated and moist, flowed into her. "For the woman you used to be, the home you left behind...."

"No," she whispered, seeking his mouth again. At the time it seemed the only true thing in the world. "No."

"Even for the man you once married?"

"That's not fair."

"Did he ever make you feel like this?"

"Stop it. Don't—"

She tried to turn her face away but his fingers tightened, holding her close, demanding an answer. Demanding the truth. "Did he?"

"No!" she gasped. She opened her eyes to the power of his, burning blue orbs blazing their way into her soul. "No, he never did, not ever! Is that what you wanted? Are you happy now?"

She wrenched her face away and he let her go. But he hooked her chin with his finger and very gently guided her to look at him again.

"Then," he said softly, "who is the fantasy?"

Gillian swallowed on an uncertain breath and found she could no longer hold his gaze. This was dangerously close to getting out of hand. This was far, far more than she had ever expected, or wanted. This was definitely not her style.

"They'll come for me, you know," she said hoarsely.

His fingertip stroked her cheek. "Who will, love?"

Gillian wanted to pull away from his caress—and she didn't. Her heart was beating crazily, with anxiety, anticipation, desire and fear—with the wild, sweet remembrance of his kisses, which still heated her blood. "They. The world. My father. He'll come for me, I know he will."

He smiled. "I shall look forward to meeting him."

Gillian swallowed hard. "I can't stay here. You know I can't."

He leaned toward her again. "Then let us make the most of the time we have."

Quickly Gillian averted her face, her heart racing wildly. "I want to go back now."

"No," he said gently, "you don't." He took her hands and stood, helping her to her feet. "But I will take you back, anyway."

Her knees were shaking; she had to hold on to his hands for balance for a moment. Nonetheless, she managed to make her voice almost steady as she said, "What do you want from me, Gabriel?"

His smile was slow, his eyes were tender. "Everything... and nothing. To be with you, to enjoy you, to adore you, to give you pleasure. For now, to court you."

Gillian drew an uneven breath. "And what, do you think, will be the result of that courtship?"

A shadow of sadness crossed his face; briefly, he dropped his eyes. "Ah," he said quietly. "That is the question, isn't it?"

They left the glade and walked again arm in arm through the corridors. After a time Gabriel began to talk of lighter things, and Gillian pretended to respond. But she knew the fantasy could not go on much longer.

She had to leave this place. Soon.

# Chapter Seven

Gillian tried to imagine the paper she would write when she returned to civilization. All of the elements for a classic study of diverted social evolution were present in this microcosm at the center of the earth, enough to make her name a household word in her field. An isolated tribe had been acted upon by Western culture and had incorporated that culture into its own with results that were fascinating, if not actually believable.

And that was the trouble. Whenever Gillian tried to put her observations into words her summation sounded more like a fantasy novel—or worse, the Hollywood interpretation of a fantasy novel—than a dissertation. Did she seriously expect anyone to believe that she had discovered an entire race of people living inside a volcano in the heart of the Andes, unexposed to the modern world yet capable of sustaining an artificially controlled climate whose mechanics Gillian had yet to figure out, of feeding themselves via means of organic gardening and an irrigation system that was, again, a mystery to her? Whose legends and customs were straight from the jungle but who were familiar with electricity and Shakespeare? Whose standard of living, life expectancy and health status rivaled that of any advanced nation in the world—but who had never even heard the *names* of most of those nations? And all of it was due to one very eccentric, completely enigmatic, thoroughly incomprehensible man.

It was quite impossible, of course, and she would be laughed out of every university in the world should she ever try to publish such a paper. But if she did not intend to prepare a study on this place, if she could not formulate some viable theory that would explain its existence and try to make that theory work for her, there was no reason for her to stay.

"And would you like to know the rest of my theory?" she said out loud to the serving woman who sat near her. The other woman only understood about half of what Gillian said—perhaps less—but Gillian had grown accustomed to engaging in one-sided conversations and even found she enjoyed them.

The woman grinned and ducked her head, and Gillian took that as an affirmative. "I think that your people are actually the descendants of the lost tribe that I came here to look for in the first place. Yes, I know, but what other explanation is there? We have evidence that a socially advanced race on level with the Maya once inhabited this area, but no evidence of what became of them . . . and here you are. So corrupted by Western influence, of course, that it's impossible to prove your antecedents. And wouldn't I love to know how *that* happened. Obviously Gabriel is not the first one to discover this place. If only I knew how old it was!"

She was in her private chambers, where she spent most of her mornings, speaking as she paced the floor. The servant sat on a low hassock, doing needlework, appearing to enjoy the flow of Gillian's monologue, even if she didn't understand the words. And her English *had* improved noticeably since she had begun to spend her spare time listening to Gillian talk. In that way, Gillian supposed she herself was adding to the corruption of this culture, but at this point it hardly seemed to matter.

Every day she felt less like an anthropologist and more like a woman—a woman who was awakening to life again after a long, drugged sleep, or a woman who was captured helplessly in the folds of an incredible dream. She hadn't really decided which it was yet.

"Listen," she said, turning to the woman, "there must be stories about the time when your people first came to this place. Can't you tell me some of them?"

She had asked before, that and other similar questions, but she never got much of an answer. Either the women's English was still too poor to understand the question, or they pretended it was. Today's response was typical.

"We are here," she answered, smiling placidly. "We are always here."

Gillian repressed her sigh of frustration. "You go outside sometimes. Some of your people must leave sometimes."

"Why?"

That was a new word for the woman and one that, in Gillian's opinion, was being greatly overused of late. Nonetheless she felt compelled to answer. There was always the chance, after all, that she actually knew what the word meant.

"Because," she explained patiently, "they might want to live in another place, or just see what's outside this place. They might want to hunt or explore. They might come back. They might not."

The woman shook her head and turned back to her needlework. "It is good here. Happy here. No one leaves. No one comes back."

Gillian looked at her thoughtfully for a moment, wondering if it were possible she was telling the truth... and then deciding that, as far as this place was concerned, anything was possible.

Gillian chose her words carefully. "Listen to me. I want you to think about the stories your mother told you, and your mother's mother. Do you know what I mean?"

She nodded, beaming enthusiastically. "The memory-tales. These I know."

"Good." Gillian paused a moment, thinking how to phrase it so that the woman would understand—or, at least, not pretend to misunderstand.

"Think about the memory-tales of the men who came from outside, before Gabriel—before Malik. Do you know those?"

She worked the slim wooden hook into the fabric, replying complacently, "There were none before Malik."

"Of course there were. He couldn't have done all this by himself. Someone had to help him."

"Only Malik," she replied simply.

"Long ago, before you were born, someone else came here," she explained as patiently as she could. "He brought other white men, perhaps, and they married the women of your tribe and had babies. They taught their children to speak the languages they spoke—English and French and Latin and Italian. Surely you must have memory-tales about that."

"Only Malik," the woman insisted serenely. She knotted her thread and held up the square of beautifully embroidered white cloth for Gillian to see. The design was intricate and abstract, reminding her in many ways of the ornamental ink work on those rare manuscripts in the library. She was ever amazed by the delicacy of the work these women were able to achieve—and by the tools they were able to manufacture to aid them.

Nonetheless, she was not in the mood to admire needlework, and she had to force herself into polite interest. "It's lovely. What is it?"

"It is for your marriage gown," replied the other woman proudly. "You like?"

Gillian's first reaction was to smile. "That's very thoughtful of you, but I'm not getting married."

She nodded, folding her work carefully. "We spend many hours to prepare. We all make pretties for your gown. We cook. We make perfume for the marriage bed. It is good."

A slow prickle of uneasiness crept down Gillian's spine. She looked closely at the woman. "And who, exactly, will I be marrying?" It was a foolish question. She already knew the answer.

"Malik."

Gillian swallowed her first hasty words, forcing herself to unclench her fists. She kept her tone deliberately neutral. "He told you that?"

The woman just smiled. "We know."

Gillian took a deep breath, and then another. Her fists tightened again. "Will you excuse me, please? I need to have a word or two with my future husband."

She strode out of the room.

GABRIEL HEARD HER COMING and was surprised to be taken off guard. It had been a long time since he had been so wrapped up in his work that the passage of time escaped him. He hadn't realized it had grown so late, that she would be up and about now. There was little surprise in the fact, however, that the work that so consumed him involved Gillian.

While the click of her footsteps made their way down the corridor and through the winding passages of his inner chamber, he wiped his paintbrush with a solvent-coated cloth and stepped back to examine the portrait. The smooth curve of her jaw, the glint of light on glossy black hair, the arch of her brow—a little too severe to be called graceful—the thoughtful green eyes. In the portrait, her lips were parted, as though caught on the verge of a smile she wasn't quite sure she understood, and her gaze was far away, almost dreamy. Yet something about the look was not right. Something in the eyes was still missing. He had been working for days to recreate it, but it was not yet perfect.

He had seen that look on her face that day at the glade and he had wanted to hold it captured in his mind forever. She might never look at him that way again. The tenderness in her eyes might turn to bitterness or hate, years might mar her skin or steal the light from her eyes. The memory of her as he wished to see her would begin to fade, as memory always did. But on the canvas she was eternal. When the portrait was finished he had only to look at what was rendered here to relive the moment, to recall how once she had enchanted him.

He placed the cover over the canvas and turned to greet her as she rounded the last corner.

Her eyes were flashing and her cheeks a little flushed with exertion; she was angry and her strides had been long. Gabriel couldn't help smiling when he saw her, for her passions were an endless source of delight to him. He tried to recall when he had last felt deeply about anything, but could not. Her capacity for expending enormous amounts of energy on trivialities never ceased to amaze him, and in some ways he envied her.

She stopped a few feet away from him, her eyes sweeping the room. She seemed surprised by the easel and palette, and she gave more than a cursory note of his attire, which was the open robe and short breeches he had worn when they'd first met. He had discovered he enjoyed changing costumes for her, and she had not seen him in such dishabille since that first night. He noticed, however, that a flicker of sexual interest—purely unconscious on her part, he was sure—crossed her expression, mitigating her anger, as her eyes moved over the bare portions of his body.

She quickly recovered her cool indignation as she met his eyes. "Forgive me for barging in," she said, "but I understand we are to be married."

That he had not expected. He lifted an eyebrow, amused. "How delightful."

"I'm sure it is. I'm also sure it will be a lovely ceremony and I should be flattered beyond words, but for future reference, most women like to be asked first!"

She was really the most captivating creature. Nothing about her was predictable or certain, everything about her was wholly refreshing. She made him feel like laughing all the time, and laughter, until she came along, was something that he had thought he had forgotten.

"At one time there was an expression among gentlemen," he said, " 'just like a woman.' I daresay it would be inappropriate to use that expression to describe you now."

She glared at him. "You would be right."

He finished cleaning the paintbrush and selected another, repeating the procedure. He never tired of looking at her. His hands had been tracing the curves and planes, shadows and lights of her face for hours, and he knew it now as he did his own—yet it was still exciting to him. Still welcome to see.

"Nonetheless," he said, "you must admit your behavior is rather embarrassingly typical for your sex. Jumping to conclusions, flinging accusations—"

"God, your arrogance is beyond belief!"

She thrust her fingers into her hair in a highly dramatized gesture of frustration. Her agitation, however, was not exaggerated, and as entertaining as it was to watch, he did not like to be accused wrongly.

"My dear, treasured girl," he said, putting the paintbrush aside, "it shall be my most extreme pleasure to wed you, if that's what you want. But it frankly wasn't my first choice. The women of this place, as is true of women everywhere, have their own agenda, and I seem to have unwittingly become the victim of it. If this makes me arrogant, I do apologize."

She glared at him for a long moment, then she said, "No. That's not what makes you arrogant. I think you were born arrogant, like some feudal lord to the manor born, and nothing in this world or any other can change that. But that's not even what I resent the most. I can't blame you for what you can't help."

He inclined his head graciously.

Her fists closed, her eyes narrowed. "What bothers me is that you think your arrogance is the only thing I have to be upset about—that some foolishness over a premature wedding is what I'm angry about."

"And it's not? Now I am confused." He turned and gestured the way beyond a curtained wall. "Will you come and sit down? I was about to take some refreshment. Have you eaten already? Shall I send for breakfast?"

"No," she said shortly. "I mean, yes. Breakfast was hours ago."

Nonetheless she followed him into an anteroom where a silver tea service was set up in the middle of a Turkish hassock. The walls were a rich cerulean blue trimmed with gold, the fabric of the wide sectioned hassock a deep underwater green. He was very far from the ocean now and sometimes he missed it. This room reminded him of the sea.

He sat casually on the hassock and reached for the teapot, which contained his own herbal blend. He gestured her to join him, but she remained standing over him, scowling.

"Please understand I'm only asking to be polite," he said, pouring the tea into a bone-china cup, "but what exactly *are* you angry about?"

He offered her the cup and she refused. He took it for himself, adding sweetener.

"How long have you been here, Gabriel?" she demanded. "Why did you come here, how did you find this place, how can you afford to stay here? How old is this place, who built it, who are these people and where did they come from? Where are *you* from and who is your family? And pardon me for seeming nosy, but I do think those are the *least* I need to know about the man an entire civilization believes I'm going to marry!"

He sipped his tea, observing her thoughtfully, wondering how long he had really expected to postpone this moment, surprised to discover he had almost managed to convince himself it would never come at all. She was right. He was arrogant. Too many years of masterfully controlling his own destiny had blinded him to the needs of others, and that was a grave mistake.

"It was never my intention to be less than honest with you, Gillian."

She looked at him measuringly. "Then be honest about this. Have you made any effort at all to contact Lima and get word to the authorities about where I am?"

He held her gaze. "No."

She took a long, uncertain breath and looked away, but not before he saw the hurt and betrayal in her eyes. "Well," she said flatly. "I should have known."

She raised her eyes to him forcefully, pressing her palms together. Her heart was pounding, slow and hard, denying the calm she forced into her words. "Fortunately for me, it doesn't matter. My father is one of the most influential men in the country and he won't believe I'm dead. He'll send a team—a dozen teams—and he won't give up until they've combed every inch of this countryside. You picked the wrong woman to try and kidnap, Mr. Malik."

His face was impassive. "You have hardly been kidnapped. I told you I had no radio."

She studied him in silence for a long time, as though seriously considering, for the first time, the possibility that he might be telling the truth. At last she said, in an odd, careful tone, "You also told me I wasn't a prisoner here."

"You're not." He wasn't entirely able to keep the impatience out of his tone. "Do you see any bars or chains? I thought you were content here."

"Content?" Incredulity sharpened her voice. "Like a bird in a cage is content? You're smarter than that, Gabriel. I may not know much about you, but I do know that."

She took a breath and squared her shoulders, making herself infinitesimally bigger in that brave way he adored. "I'm strong enough to travel," she said firmly. "There's nothing for me to do here, my research has come to a dead end and heaven knows you're no help. It's time for me to go."

He smiled and set his cup aside. "So you've been researching us, have you?"

She looked a little uncomfortable. "Of course. Research is what I do."

"And that's the only thing that has kept you here."

She looked for a moment as though she might lie, then admitted, "No. It was exciting, fascinating. It's not every day a person stumbles on Shangri-la in the middle of the Andes. Of course I enjoyed it."

"And me? Didn't you enjoy me—even a little?"

Frustration and pain flashed in her eyes. "What do you want me to say? Yes, I enjoyed being treated like a princess! Yes, your kisses make my head spin! Yes, I'll dream about you for years to come! But that's all it is, okay? A dream! So if you think your sex appeal—undeniable though it may be—is all it takes to make me want to stay, you can just think again. I have a life!"

He smiled and slowly stood up. "I see." He reached out to touch her shoulder, and she shrugged away.

"Don't touch me." She scowled at him. "What do you see?"

"That you're afraid."

Again she was incredulous. "Of you?"

"Of you. And of what you might begin to feel for me if you stayed much longer."

This time she said nothing. She merely stared at him, eyes wide with the turmoil of emotion that battled inside her.

For a moment he thought he might have pushed too far, demanded too much too soon, or that he might even be wrong. It disturbed him to realize how very much he did *not* want to be wrong about this woman.

"That's absurd," she said shortly.

He waited. She slid a quick assessing glance toward him and seemed to reconsider.

"All right," she said after a moment. Her voice was tight. "I'm more attracted to you than to any man I've ever met, and I think you know that. And yes, there's a good chance that if I stay much longer that attraction will turn into something a lot deeper. But that's not what frightens me. What frightens me is you—because you don't fit into any of the niches of my life, because you can't be defined, because you don't make *sense*.

"I don't know you, I can't begin to figure you out, and if someone asked me to describe you in one sentence I couldn't even do that. But you make me feel . . ." And then she caught her breath, almost as though to keep her voice from breaking with sudden emotion. "Too much," she finished simply. "You make me feel too much."

Gabriel had not expected her to say that. From the beginning he had been enchanted by her, amused by her, intrigued by her and had pursued her for the joy of pursuit. He had wanted her with the simple elemental greed that a collector such as he wanted anything that struck him as rare and beautiful, and he had expected the conquest to be sweet. He had never intended to hurt her or confuse her or diminish her in any way.

Now it appeared he had done all those things, and it made him angry to see the pain in her eyes. Had it been so long since he had cared what went on inside another human being that he had forgotten others beside himself could suffer? Could he truly have grown so callous?

Those were questions he wasn't prepared to answer, hadn't expected to *have* to answer. He didn't want to deal with this.

"I'm sorry if my attentions inconvenienced you," he said. "That was not my intention."

"What *was* your intention?" she insisted. "You saved my life, you brought me here to the farthest reaches of nowhere, you try to seduce me with your charm and your wit and your sex appeal...but what did you expect would come from it? What did you want from me, anyway?"

She was the master of the feminine brand of torture. She would push and push until she pushed him over the edge. How dare she challenge him in such a fashion? How dare she test the limits of his charity?

He returned to his tea, mostly to hide from her his rising annoyance. His voice was cool. "Why, to make you a slave to my sexual appetites, of course. To use you until I grew tired of you and then toss you into a dungeon somewhere to rot."

Gillian stared at him. She had never heard him speak like that before; certainly she had not expected the conversation to take this course when she entered the room. Perhaps she should have backed down. Perhaps she should have just turned and left the room and approached him again when he was in a better mood. But she had too much at stake to do that. Not only her physical freedom but emotions she had only begun to tap, things she had never expected to feel again, were held in the palm of Gabriel's strong hand. She had to have some answers.

Her voice was a little muffled with the effort to hold back her hurt as she replied, "I was serious."

Her tone only exacerbated Gabriel's irritation. It seemed to him suddenly she was constantly demanding from him things he was incapable of giving, that no matter what he did for her it would never be enough. Anger and frustration churned inside him.

"You are always serious," he replied sharply. "Always the Pandora, asking your ceaseless troublemaking questions. Why can't you simply let things be?''

Gillian's own temper was beginning to rise in response to his, and she struggled to keep her voice even. "You know the answer to that."

Gabriel sipped the tea, though it had grown cold and tasted like bile in his throat. "I know nothing except I am sick to death of being analyzed and dissected and questioned on every move I make, every detail of my existence. That's not why I brought you here."

Gillian had sought a confrontation, yes, but she had never expected it to go like this. She had never expected to lose control. Yet with every word he spoke, she was reminded just how insignificant was the role she played in her own destiny, and the colder his anger got, the hotter her own grew.

Her fists tightened at her sides. "Why *did* you bring me here?"

HE SHOT HER A GLANCE that was as hot as coals, though his face remained immobile and his voice perfectly smooth. "Forgive me, I was seized by some misguided impulse to save your life. I see now it was a mistake."

"My God," she breathed. "You *are* arrogant."

"Yes," he returned coldly. Though his tone and his expression were like ice, the fire of fury burned in his veins. He hated her, he hated himself, and the worst of it was he couldn't begin to tell why. "I'm arrogant, I'm cruel, I'm judgmental and domineering and a dozen—a hundred—more unpleasant things you have yet to discover. I've made a lifelong study of vice, I've perfected corruption to an art form, and you would be amazed at how self-absorbed and ruthless I can be.''

"I doubt that. I don't think anything you could do would amaze me anymore.''

"Continue to provoke me," he said harshly, "and you will find out.''

Gillian's hand went to her throat. It was an instinctive gesture of self-protection she wasn't even aware of making, but his eyes blazed when he saw it. Quickly, angrily, he looked away.

Her voice was hoarse and low. "I have misjudged you.''

"I can't think how that can be possible when only a moment ago you were all atwitter because you didn't know anything about me. Or could it be, my dear Miss Aldair, that you have leapt to conclusions?''

He finished off the tea and set the cup and saucer down with a rattle. Without those vestments of civilization in his hands he felt untamed, a beast in the drawing room, on the verge of chaos. He was furious with her for making him feel that way, for reminding him of what he had been...could be again.

He did not have to tolerate this kind of discord in his own house. Blast it all, he *would* not tolerate it.

"Phillipe was right," he said shortly, without looking at her. "You don't belong here. Kindly leave me in peace."

"I'd be happy to! That's all I've wanted since I got here."

He turned on her, the folds of his robe billowing around him, his blue eyes glittering. "Not all."

The softness of his tone held more menace than a shout would have done. Suddenly he seemed very large to her, enormously powerful, and when he looked at her she wanted to take a step backward. Pride and sheer willpower kept her rooted to the spot.

"Tell me you haven't enjoyed it, Gillian," he insisted silkily. "The seductive games we've played, the little flirtations, the fantasies, the unspoken promises. Tell me I haven't given you more in a few spare days than all the other pale excuses for men you've known in your lifetime. That you haven't felt more a woman with me than you have since reaching puberty and that you haven't delighted in every moment of it. Can you tell me that, Gillian?"

Gillian wanted to whirl and stalk away from him in righteous indignation, to demolish him with a few well-chosen words, perhaps to punctuate the whole with a slap in the face. But it was anger and disappointment, irrational as both those emotions might be under the circumstances, that made her hold his gaze, that made her reply spitefully, "Enjoyed it? Why it's been a dream come true. What woman wouldn't want to be part of your oh-so-well-trained harem?''

"What?"

She must have seen the warning signs, the slight loss of color, the tightening around his lips. She simply chose to ignore them. Her fists tightened at her sides. "Let's stop the game-playing, okay? You have sex with those girls, don't you? How else can you explain the mixed-race children? The only thing I don't understand is why you'd even bother trying to 'court' a woman like me—as you so quaintly put it—when all you have to do is beckon to have them lined up to do your bidding. Unfortunately for you, I'm not quite so impressionable!''

"Aren't you?"

A quiet had come over him—his voice, his stance, his face—that practically screamed danger. Only his eyes remained on fire, and this time when he took a step toward her she did move back, but to no avail. He caught her shoulders with a quickness and a strength that made her muffle a cry of surprise. He pulled her against him roughly.

"Do you find me so resistible, Gillian?" His thighs were like columns of stone against hers, his breath seared her face. "Do you think it would be so easy to walk away from me if I didn't want you to?"

She tried to twist away, but with an iron grip he caught the arms that would have pushed against his chest. His voice was not much above a whisper, but it went through her like an electric current through water, as effortlessly and as effectively as his eyes bored into her soul.

"Shall I show you just how impressionable you are, Gillian?" His voice was low and seductive, almost a whisper. "I have forgotten more about pleasuring a woman than most men will ever know in their lifetimes. Shall I show you, Gillian? Shall I call my girls to massage your skin with ancient oils that will have you writhing with desire? Shall I demonstrate just exactly how I can strip away your will an inch at a time until you are begging for release?

"I can make you want me, Gillian," he continued. "I can bring you to your knees with wanting me, I can make you weep for wanting me. And you know that's true, don't you?"

Her heart was pounding, shaking in her chest, roaring in her ears, and she could not move her eyes from his. *Yes...yes, I know....* And in that moment, poised on the brink of discovery, it seemed to Gillian that the answer to all her questions were just within her reach. A breath away, a kiss away, a long and desperate embrace away...for she did want him, all of him, body and soul, with a helpless, desperate surrender that was unlike anything she had ever known before. And that terrified her, enraged her, filled her with tumult.

"You are a monster."

His hands tightened on her arms, for one brief and terrible moment, with a bruising force, and the anger that flared in his eyes was filled with such pain, such surprise, that Gillian automatically flinched back from it; she wanted to reach out and grab her words out of the air, but it was too late.

He released her with an abruptness that caused her to stumble backward. "Get out of here," he said roughly, "before we are both sorry."

This time Gillian did not hesitate. She turned and ran.

# Chapter Eight

For a long time after her running footsteps died away, Gabriel stood as still as a statue in the center of the room, silently cursing himself and her in every language he knew. Then he turned abruptly and strode into the other room and, spying the covered canvas still in place on the easel, he lifted his arm and swept it to the floor. In the process, his sleeve caught the edge of the table that held the painting supplies and sent it crashing to the floor. Jars of paint exploded, brushes flew across the room, paint and solvent splattered the floor and walls.

The clatter sounded like an explosion in the stone chamber, a cacophony of rage and violence that was out of place here, unwelcome to his ears. It startled Gabriel out of most of his anger. When he became aware that Phillipe was standing quietly near the entryway watching, very little was left of his tantrum except shame.

Gabriel pushed back his hair with his hand, drawing a long slow breath. His voice sounded a little hoarse when he spoke. "I'm sorry you had to see that." The words were stiff. "I can't remember the last time I acted so childishly. I thought I was beyond such behavior."

Phillipe stepped forward and righted the overturned table, setting a single unbroken jar on top of it. "Females have been known to bring out the worst in men."

"Yes," agreed Gabriel dully. Suddenly he felt exhausted, wrung out by the onslaught of unfamiliar emotions. What had happened? How had it started? How had it gotten so out of hand?

There was a cushioned bench in one corner of the room; he walked to it and sat down heavily, stretching out his legs before him. "And to think only moments earlier," he muttered, mostly to himself, "I was envying her passions. But they are contagious, and not very attractive on me, I'm afraid."

He leaned his head back against the wall, regarding Phillipe through half-lowered lashes. "Ah, old friend," he said quietly, "life is complex, isn't it? I think I am beginning to recall why I've found it so comfortable to live alone."

Phillipe stood several feet away, his hands folded inside the full sleeves of his robe, his round face betraying no censure. He reminded Gabriel of a priest, and he supposed the role of confessor was one Gabriel had called upon his friend to play far too often in the past.

Phillipe said, "Sometimes it seems the things we want most are the things that bring the most pain."

Gabriel frowned a little, uncomfortable with the understanding that was coming upon him. That he wanted her was a given. He had wanted her from the first moment and he had made no secret about it. What disturbed him was that until today he had not realized how *much* he wanted her.

Or perhaps it was simply that she represented one of the few things in this world he could not have.

"Sometimes your wisdom astounds me, Phillipe."

Phillipe smiled. "I have had a good teacher."

Gabriel got to his feet. "I should go after her."

But Phillipe extended a hand to stop him, lightly touching his arm as he started to move past. "And tell her what?"

Gabriel hesitated, once again surprised at how muddled his thinking had become in such a short time. Indeed, tell her what? The truth? That was beyond consideration. And yet the truth was all she had asked from him from the moment she had regained consciousness and come to seek him out in his chamber.

For a long time he simply stared at Phillipe, not knowing what to say. Then he gave a small shake of his head and released a breath that sounded a great deal like a sigh. "And now I suppose I must admit you were right from the beginning, Phillipe. I never should have brought her here."

Phillipe returned his gaze sympathetically. "What are you going to do?" he asked.

But for the first time in a very long time, Gabriel didn't know.

GILLIAN WAS MIDWAY DOWN the labyrinthian corridor when she realized she was acting like a fool. She had fled from him as though he were wielding a knife, and Gillian Aldair didn't run away from any man. What was the matter with her, anyway? What was she *really* running from?

She slowed her steps, embarrassed to find that her breath was coming in unsteady gulps. The man had saved her life, had treated her with nothing but kindness, and she had repaid him with demands and accusations. She had quite a bit to be embarrassed about.

He was right. For all his maddening secrecy and persistent intrigue, it was not Gabriel she was afraid of, but the way he made her feel. Yes, he brought disorder. Yes, he brought mystery and irrationality and all the things she had dedicated her life to conquering, but those things were not the worst of what he did to her. The worst of it was the emotions he stirred inside her, the ashes of feelings she had thought long dead that he now fanned to life. She wasn't ready for those feelings, not now, not with him. Certainly not with him.

She didn't even know him, and what she did know about him worried her. He lived in an underground chamber in the middle of the Andes, completely cut off from civilization. He had no visible means of support but surrounded himself with incredible luxuries. He could quote the classics in their original languages and spoke familiarly of architecture, archaeology and physics, but had never heard of skateboards and thought jeeps were only used by the military. He was a study in contrasts and contradictions, and any of of those contradictions would have been enough to alarm any sensible woman. Yet this man had made her feel things she had never felt for anyone before...including Jerry. That was what frightened her.

It was good for people to be shaken up every once in a while, her father said. She had never agreed with him on that. Not ever.

She stopped and rested one shoulder against the wall, taking a moment to get her bearings, literally and figuratively. "Damn," she muttered out loud. She hated to be wrong, and she had been very wrong in her behavior with Gabriel.

So what was she going to do now?

Maybe, she reasoned slowly, she would do well to start with trying to figure out what she *wanted*. And the first thing she wanted was not to have Gabriel angry with her.

She turned and began to retrace her steps.

All her life had been carefully arranged, perfectly predictable, steady and safe. She had walked away from adventure to marry Jerry. She had turned down fieldwork for a teaching assignment at a mediocre university. She was good at what she did and she knew her work, but the truth was that if her tenure had not been at stake she might not even have accepted the dig that had brought her here. All of her adventures were safe and manufactured, and she had always liked it that way. But Gabriel . . . he was none of those things. He was the first genuine adventure of her life, and maybe the second thing she wanted was to see where this might lead.

She still wanted answers, and she would find them. But the maxim that cautioned against throwing the baby out with the bathwater was appropriate here. Just because Gabriel was a part of this mystery did not mean he was the cause of it. And she would be beyond foolish to throw away what might well be her only chance at something incredibly special just because it frightened her a little.

She had walked quite a way before she realized she must have taken a wrong turn, either on her way out or on her way back. She cursed herself again for not paying closer attention. It was going to be difficult enough to apologize to Gabriel without getting lost in the process.

She did not remember going through the stone archway that set apart Gabriel's suite, so she assumed she must still be in his apartment. She had never realized it was so big before. There were two doorways ahead, either one of which might lead her back to more familiar surroundings—or cause her to be even more hopelessly lost. She took the door to the left.

The automatic lights came up as she moved through the door, and she saw immediately this was a closed room, with no exit on the other side that might lead her into more familiar territory. She started to leave, but something about the room caught her attention, inciting her curiosity. The arrangement of long smooth tables and countertops, the sophisticated though unfamiliar-looking stainless-steel equipment, the tall cabinets fronted in opaque black glass... And then she saw the stand of beakers, test-tube racks and pipettes, and it struck her suddenly. This was a laboratory.

She moved inside cautiously, fighting the dread that had begun to prickle at the pit of her stomach. The counters and tabletops were obsidian, there were high benches instead of stools, the customary collection of microscopes and centrifuges were missing. But Gillian had been in enough laboratories in her lifetime to recognize one when she saw it.

She told herself it wasn't all that unusual. Hadn't Gabriel told her once he was a doctor? She hadn't entirely believed him, but there was no law against having a laboratory in his house.

What bothered her was that she couldn't identify any of the equipment. There was a device pushed back against the wall of one of the counters that might have been an electron microscope, except it was sleeker, smaller and far more compact than the ones she had seen. Another cylindrical device bathed a collection of glass slides in what appeared to be a low-level infrared light. A square, obsidian-fronted container was warm to the touch; it might have been an incubator.

Gillian stood in the center of the room, puzzled and uneasy, and unable to say exactly why. Certainly she had seen many stranger things since coming to this place. Why, then, was she suddenly seized by an urge to turn and leave this room as fast as she possibly could, before... Before she discovered something she really didn't want to know.

But even as that terrible certainty gripped her, an equally commanding drive took over. He had called her Pandora, and Gillian remembered very well what had become of that hapless lady. But she could no more subdue her basic nature than stop the wind or master the rain. While every instinct inside her screamed at her to leave, to walk away now and not look back, Gillian moved to one of the cabinets and opened it.

Pandora's box could not have held more trouble, and yet in some dread and fascinated way, Gillian was almost unsurprised. The cabinet was filled with rows of jars and vials, all neatly labeled in Latin. Gillian's Latin was rudimentary and many of labels she could not interpret. Others—the narcotics, mostly—were perfectly clear. Gabriel Malik had set himself up a home pharmaceutical lab, and she was quite certain that what came out of it was illegal in most countries of the world.

Drugs. It was, after all, as simple as that.

Gillian supposed she had always known that someone had to manufacture the poisons that made their way to the streets, killing children and provoking ordinary citizens into lives of depravity and crime, but it was not something to which she had ever given much thought. One could not work on a college campus and remain unaware of the drug problem in the United States, nor pretend ignorance of its consequences. But it had never personally touched her life. Until now.

Feeling like a character in her own bad dream, Gillian reached forward and removed one of the bottles from the shelf. She lifted the lid and examined the contents cautiously. It was a brownish substance whose texture and odor were unfamiliar to her; it could have been a perfectly harmless dried herb, or the basis for a new hallucinogen. She shook out a few crystals onto the back of her hand for a better look. Almost immediately the skin where the substance touched began to tingle and grow numb. She cursed softly and blew the material off her skin.

"Stupid," she whispered. "Stupid, stupid, stupid." But she did not know whether that was an epithet for her own gullibility or for Gabriel's involvement in the world's most heinous commerce.

She felt sickened, and her reaction was an odd combination of repulsion for what she had found and disappointment for the utter mundanity of it. Drugs. She had been right from the beginning. Gabriel was nothing more than a common, ordinary, garden-variety drug dealer.

Her lips tightened into a grim line as she looked at the bottle in her hand. For one wild moment she was seized by the impulse to confront Gabriel with it, to demand an explanation, and she made herself stand still, her fingers tightening around the bottle until the knuckles grew white, until the impulse passed.

She returned the bottle to the shelf and closed the cabinet softly, her heart beating with a heavy, sluggish rhythm. She had seen the evidence with her own eyes, confirmation of her first, instinctive suspicions about him, yet still there was a part of her that balked at accepting the truth. Some small relentless part that insisted something about this wasn't right, that wanted to hear whatever explanation he might invent, that desperately clung to the fantasy she had created in her own mind.

But she hadn't completely abandoned her common sense. She knew that the moment she had opened that cabinet door everything had changed. Millions, even billions, of dollars could be at stake in this enterprise, and in this business people made their own rules. She would be a fool to confront Gabriel with this, or to let anyone know what she had discovered. As for what she was to do now—there simply wasn't any choice.

She couldn't stay here another minute. Someone might have seen her come in here; she might have left traces of her presence she was too upset to see. Even now evidence of her subterfuge might be making its way to Gabriel. What might he do when he found out? She didn't want him to have to make that decision. She didn't want to know what that decision might be.

She had to find a way out of this place. Now.

GABRIEL PICKED UP the portrait and examined it for damage. There was a scrape in the upper left corner and some smearing of the dark shades of the hair, but nothing beyond repair. He set the painting on the easel and his gaze was drawn once again to the eyes. He tried to envision the expression he had wanted to capture there, but all he could see was that trapped, angry look.

He covered the canvas again.

"I think," Phillipe offered in a musing tone, "these females on the outside are much different from the ones we know. You would find in the end she is too much trouble to keep."

That made Gabriel smile in spite of himself. "It seems to me that has been true of females from the beginning of time. And that's exactly what makes them so impossible to resist."

But the smile faded as he lifted his arm to touch the covered canvas again, as though debating whether or not to uncover the face that haunted him so. "Before she came," he said thoughtfully, "I believed myself content. I had resigned myself to my lot. I'll admit, at first I saw her as a diversion, an entertainment to pass the hours, but soon she became more than that. She showed me what was missing in my life, and she made me want to fill it. Nothing can undo that now, Phillipe. You do understand, don't you?"

Phillipe's expression was grave, and for a moment he didn't reply. Then he said quietly, "I understand. But I suspect you have survived worse."

The muscles of Gabriel's jaw tightened briefly and he dropped his arm. "Yes," he said flatly. "I have survived worse. But that doesn't make it any easier. And it doesn't mean I shall enjoy doing so again."

For a time Phillipe was again at a loss for words, and the silence was heavy in the air. Then he said simply, "I'll send someone to straighten the chamber." And with the words, he seemed to acknowledge there was nothing either of them could do at present to remedy the situation that confronted them—perhaps not ever.

Gabriel pulled himself out of his own dark thoughts with an effort, and after a moment focused on Phillipe. "No," he said, and turned from the canvas. "I'll do it."

Gabriel began picking up the broken jars and scattered brushes, and Phillipe started for the door. They were both arrested by the distant high-pitched squeal of an alarm. It had been so long since Gabriel had heard that sound that for a moment he did not recognize it. Phillipe had never heard it, and he turned to Gabriel with a question on his face.

"It's the safety alert," Gabriel said suddenly. "In the old part of the tunnels." He looked at Phillipe. "Is someone working there?"

Phillipe shook his head. "No one is authorized to be in that part of the structure. Why would anyone want to—"

But already Gabriel was pushing past him, and the answer was clear on his face.

He moved swiftly to the console in the central chamber and called up the monitor. When the screen appeared, he disengaged the alarm and requested its source. In less than a second the image appeared.

"Gillian," he whispered. "No."

For a moment horror left him rooted to the spot, but it felt like hours before the strength returned to his legs, the focus to his muscles. He turned at a half run toward the door.

"Malik!"

Phillipe caught his arm. Gabriel looked at him in impatient confusion.

"Let her go," Phillipe said quietly.

"Are you crazy?" Gabriel pulled his arm away. "She's going to kill herself!"

Once again Phillipe's hand closed around his arm, harder this time. He repeated with quiet, forceful deliberation, "Let her go."

Gabriel looked into his old friend's eyes and saw something there he had never expected to see—something he could not, at that moment, even believe he was seeing. And because he couldn't believe it, because he had no time to waste on trying, he simply refused to acknowledge it.

He pulled forcefully from Phillipe's grip and ran from the room.

LOOKING BACK, Gillian could catalog her mistakes one by one, and almost in the order she made them.

Her first mistake, of course, was impetuosity. She should have taken a moment to think it through, to consider all the evidence, to use the skills of logic and reason she spent so much time trying to instill in her students year after year. Perhaps if the fight with Gabriel had not taken place, if she had not been at such a high emotional pitch, she might have done so, and the conclusion she reached about the strange laboratory might have been a very different one indeed.

Even so, the sane and rational person she had been when she left her safe and comfortable home for unexplored regions of South America would never have ventured out unprepared. Even the foolhardy trek that had brought her here—and almost cost her her life—had not been undertaken without painstaking preparation. At the very least she should have put together a survival pack. She did not even change her shoes.

In truth, Gillian hadn't planned on making her escape at that moment. She didn't really plan anything. When she finally made her way out of the labyrinth of corridors, with her head still clamoring in horror and confusion and her heart aching in her chest, she discovered herself on the promenade that led to the meadow overlook. Instead of turning back toward her own rooms, she followed the boulevard upward.

Perhaps she was only looking to clear her thoughts. Perhaps she instinctively sought the place where she had always been happiest with Gabriel. Or perhaps in the back of her mind even then a plan was forming, ill-conceived though it might be. Whatever her justification, the truth was that in her current state of mind she should not have set out to explore.

When she came to the narrow stairs that led up to the ledge from which Gabriel had first shown her the panorama of greenery below, she took them. The backs of her thighs ached, and she clung to the wall for support as she struggled upward, finally reaching the ledge where daylight spilled downward like misty rain, widening its scope as it did. She stood there, leaning against the rock wall and breathing hard, hoping that some of her anger and hurt might be dissipated by the exertion. It wasn't. That was

when she looked up and saw that the stairs continued beyond the ledge.

She had never noticed this before, because the artificial lighting ended at the edge and the remainder
of the stairway was in shadow. Toward the top of the
cylinder, where the sunlight was strongest, she could
see the iron handholds and, in places, even the re-
mains of what might have been scaffolding. Gabriel
had told her the scaffolding did not lead to an exit,
and she supposed in some part of her mind she *did*
believe him. But the other part of her had to see for
itself.

She started up the stairs.

She was reminded of a castle tower as she as-
cended into darkness, hugging the stone wall for
safety. There was an echo effect as she climbed
higher; sounds from below were eerily clear—mur-
muring voices, shuffling feet, the clang of tools that
made up the everyday life of this place. The air
seemed dank, and she realized she had left behind the
artificial environment that made life below so pleasant. The walls were slippery with moisture, and more
than once her feet—clad only in light cloth slip-
pers—came close to missing a step, for the treads
grew narrower and farther apart as she climbed, until it was almost like ascending a ladder.

Eventually the stairs deteriorated into little more
than indentations carved from the rock face, and she
spotted the first of the iron rings that had once been
used as handholds by some long-ago workmen. She

paused, gasping for breath, clinging to the iron ring
with one hand and the rock face with the other, and
she thought, *This is insane. You're going to get
yourself killed. Turn around and go back before you
fall....*

And that was exactly what she might have done, if
she had not heard footsteps rushing up the stairs after her.

She felt like a fly clinging to the side of the wall.
She couldn't go back. She was terrified to look
down. There was nothing for her to do but go on,
and where that might lead her she couldn't begin to
guess.

She grasped the iron ring and pulled herself up,
seeking a foothold in the rough stone wall. Her heart
was pounding, now as much from fear as exertion,
and all she could think was that she had to keep
moving, she had to put as much distance between
herself and the approaching footsteps as possible. If
she had only stopped for a moment, forced herself to
stop and think, she would have realized that panic
was her worst enemy. But the footsteps were getting
closer, and all she could really think about was a
hand snatching out to grab her ankle, pulling her
from her precarious position against the wall and
sending her tumbling into the abyss below. So she
kept moving.

That was perhaps her biggest mistake of all.

She pulled herself along by means of another
handhold, and another. As she climbed higher, the

sun overhead began to illuminate her way, and she could feel its warmth on her face. The thought of how high she must be terrified her, and over and over she had to fight the deadly urge to look down. Instead she focused on what was ahead, and she saw the first portion of the wooden scaffolding come into view.

That was the first time she realized that she was really going to escape from this place. The scaffolding was still intact, for the most part, all the way up the side of the wall. She could see it now, leading upward to the rim, all the way out of the opening in the rock, into the sky. If she could reach the scaffolding, her climb would be over; all she would have to do was walk out.

"Gillian!"

It was Gabriel's voice, echoing up at her. With all the willpower at her command, she refused to turn her head, desperate as she was to know how far he was behind her, needful as she was to see his face one more time. She pulled herself up another step.

"Gillian!" he called again. "By all that is holy, what are you doing? Stop!"

She heard a faint clanging sound and thought he was following her on the iron rings. She wanted to look back.

She couldn't look back.

"Are you insane? Whatever the matter is, it's not worth your life! For God's sake, turn back!"

There was real urgency in his voice, a touch of genuine fear. But the scaffolding was just ahead. She could reach it; she knew she could.

As much to bolster her courage as to defy him, she cried, "I'm leaving here, Gabriel, and you can't stop me! I won't let you!"

"Gillian listen to me!"

His voice sounded closer. She could hear his breath, heavy with exertion but not nearly as ragged as hers.

"Just stop one minute and listen to me! This is not the way out!"

"I'm not listening to any more of your lies! You're not doing that to me again! The scaffolding goes all the way to the top, I can see it!"

"It's an illusion! Gillian, don't do this! Turn around and look at me!"

But she had reached the scaffolding. Laboriously she pulled herself onto the wooden platform, holding on to one of the thin uprights for support. A great many of the uprights were missing, and only now could she see how old the wood beneath her feet looked, how dry and fragile.

"Gillian, stop please! That platform is thousands of years old! It can't support you!"

She knew he was telling the truth. Even if the fear in his voice had not told her so, her own eyes would have assured her that the chances of making it all the way to the top on this scaffolding were slim indeed. It might not be thousands of years old, but it was hundreds at least. There were gaps in the planks and the entire structure had begun to pull away from the wall in places. *Don't be stupid, Gillian. For once in your life, don't be stupid....*

She took a step forward, and another. It was the fourth step before she heard a board crack beneath her feet. She flung herself back against the wall, her heart pounding so hard it hurt her throat. For a moment the silence was profound, and she knew that Gabriel had stopped moving, stopped even breathing.

Then he said, very softly, "Gillian. Come back. Please."

Gillian opened her eyes. Her breathing was so ragged it sounded like sobs catching in her throat. She turned around to face him.

Gabriel was at the edge of the scaffolding, his feet still supported by rock steps, holding on to the iron ring for balance. He could have stepped onto the platform but he didn't, perhaps because he feared his extra weight would be all it would take to send them both plunging down the wall. He extended his free hand to her.

"Come back," he commanded gently.

She wanted to. More than anything in her life, she wanted to trust him, to reach out her hand and place it in his, to let him rescue her.

She pressed her closed fists against the wall and she said shakily, "I almost fell in love with you, you bastard."

Surprise flickered across his eyes, and something else—wonder, or joy—something she wanted to recapture, to hold on to, to believe in. But her own fear blinded her, and when she looked again it was gone.

He said, "And is the prospect of loving me so distasteful you would try to destroy yourself?"

"Damn you." Her voice was hoarse, still choked with anger and despair. How could she look at his face—so strong, so kind, so wise beyond his years—and believe what she knew to be true? How could she bear believing it?

"You lied to me," she said. "I almost think I could understand the rest, but you *lied.*"

Now there was caution in his face. "Could we have this conversation another time, Gillian?"

"No!"

And in that moment she knew she was about to make the biggest mistake of her life. Her back was against the wall, literally; if she went forward she would surely die, if she went back her chances weren't much better. Nonetheless a calm came over her as she held his gaze steadily. "I've seen the lab, Gabriel."

No comprehension registered in his eyes.

"What are you manufacturing?" she demanded. "Crack cocaine? Ecstasy? PCP? Probably a whole list of things I've never even heard of. The recreational drugs of the next generation are probably percolating away in there as we speak!"

He looked uncertain. "Is that why you're angry at me? Because you've seen something in my lab you don't like? I told you I was a man of medicine, Gillian. How did you imagine I kept those people healthy without the use of pharmaceuticals?"

For a moment she faltered, but only because she wanted so badly to believe in his innocence. "There were enough narcotics in there to keep an entire nation stoned for a week!"

"Perhaps." But his tone expressed little interest and his eyes moved anxiously over the scaffolding beneath her feet, the precarious tilt of the wooden railing over her head. "Also antibiotics, anti-inflammatories, live and killed viruses and a whole host of other helpful items that I really wouldn't expect you to recognize. Gillian, please come here. I can get you down safely but I can't reach you from there. Give me your hand."

Though her mind was in turmoil, the hesitation she felt betrayed her true feelings. She looked at him and she did not see a drug dealer. She did not see a criminal of any kind, or even a liar. She saw only a man who had begun to open up a whole new world for her, a world that was vast and important and rich with possibilities ... and she wanted to believe him. With all her heart, she wanted to believe him.

Nonetheless, she did not know what she might have done then—whether she would have reached for his hand or turned the other way. She never got a chance to find out. As she stood there, aching and uncertain, the boards beneath her feet abruptly shifted.

Gillian cried out and flung herself toward Gabriel. He leapt onto the edge of the scaffolding and swept her into his arms just as the boards on which she had been standing tumbled down through the pool of sunlight. She was pinned painfully for a moment between the rock wall and Gabriel's hard chest, and the wall scraped her shoulder as he pushed her past him toward the edge of the scaffolding.

"Quickly!" he commanded into her ear. "It can't hold both of us."

She was still shaking, but he gave her no chance to recover. He took her hand and placed it firmly around the first iron ring, holding her waist as she fumbled for a foothold. There was another cracking sound, and she smothered a cry as her feet finally found the shallow steps.

"Hurry!" Gabriel said.

There was yet another cracking, tearing sound from the scaffolding, and Gillian's breath sounded like sobs as she struggled to find the next hand- and footholds, slipping, catching herself, moving downward.

Still moving down, Gillian looked up to see Gabriel reach for the handhold she had just vacated. And then everything seemed to happen in slow motion. In horror she watched as, with the sound of rotting timbers and tearing metal, the entire edge of the scaffolding pulled away from the wall. Gabriel grabbed the iron ring and swung his feet off the collapsing boards, and she thought everything was going to be all right, that they both would escape unharmed. And then she saw that he was holding on with only hand. Just as he was turning to gain a more secure purchase, Gillian saw the jagged edge of a falling beam swing toward him. It struck him in the chest, tearing a gash from breast to abdomen, flinging him back against the wall. The iron ring was torn from his grasp.

The last thing Gillian saw was the surprise on his face as he fell past her into the abyss. She heard her own scream, saw her hand reaching toward him, but neither could save him. He struck the ledge below and was still.

## Chapter Nine

Gillian scrambled down the stairs toward him. She did not lose her purchase until she reached the tower staircase, and then she slid halfway down, bouncing against the wall, tripping and righting herself and stumbling again, not even feeling the pain of her bruises. She reached the ledge sobbing, half crawling, and thinking, *At least the ledge broke his fall. At least he didn't hit the bottom,* which was insane because the ledge was solid stone and more than a hundred feet down. There was no way he could have survived the fall.

He lay on his back where he had fallen, still and broken. The gaping wound caused by the ragged beam transecting his torso had bathed his skin with blood; he lay in a pool of it.

Gillian had seen accidents before. She had seen injury and even death. Never before had she seen the crushed and bleeding body of someone she cared for, knowing that she was the cause of the accident. For a moment she almost couldn't go any farther.

And then she heard a muffled moan.

In the seconds it took her to crawl to Gabriel, she made a thousand bargains with God. *Just one miracle... I didn't mean to accuse him wrongly.... I'll never doubt him again.... Don't make him pay for my curiosity and impulsiveness.... Just one miracle, please....*

She reached him with her limbs shaking so badly she could hardly see, gasping breaths choking in her throat, but there was no mistake—he was alive. For how long, she couldn't know, but his eyes were open and he was breathing, shallowly and with obvious pain.

She cradled his head in her arms. "Oh God, Gabriel," she whispered, "I'm so sorry. Hold on, please...."

He tried to say something, but the words were unclear. His eyes, those beautiful, soul-seeing eyes, were dazed and fogged over, and looking at them tore Gillian's heart in two. She had to turn away lest all the tears that were backing up in her chest and flooding her throat spill over, and she didn't want him to see that. She wanted to be brave; she didn't want his last memory of her to be of her in tears.

Gillian moved quickly to try to tend his wound, but she quickly saw it was hopeless. She bunched up the folds of his robe and pressed it against the wound, but it was soaked through with blood in seconds. She tried to think, tried to make herself calm, but her thoughts chased themselves around like frantic squirrels in a cage. She couldn't move him. She could never get him back down to the living area. If she left him to get help, he might not survive her absence. *Oh, God, don't do this. Don't make me lose him, too....*

"Gabriel," she said, whispering because she didn't have enough breath for anything stronger. "I've got to go get help." She folded a clean section of his robe, pressing it against the wound. "I'll be back. You're going to be okay. I—"

"Gillian," he said softly.

She looked at him and thought she saw the faintest touch of a tender smile on his lips. He lifted a bloody hand and touched her cheek. "Don't trouble yourself."

The tears spilled over. She tried not to sob, but she couldn't hold back the tears. She took his hand in both of hers and pressed it against her lips. "Gabriel," she said thickly, "what I said before—I didn't mean it. I only—I was ready to believe the worst because I had to believe *something*. I had to have some answers about you and—and it seems sometimes the worst is all I ever get. Oh God, Gabriel, forgive me. I was wrong, I was scared, I was stupid."

Tears splashed on his fingers; she tasted salt in her mouth. "Why did you come after me?" she whispered. "Oh, God, you should have let me go."

"I couldn't do that. You were in danger."

And then, tightening his lips against the pain, he removed his hand from her grasp and used it to brace himself. Gillian watched in amazement as he struggled to pull himself into a sitting position.

She didn't know whether to try to force him down again or help him sit up, but when she reached for him, he pushed her hand away. "No." His tone was grim. "I need no help."

"Gabriel . . ."

In alarm she reached for him again, but stopped in midmotion as her eyes fell on the bloody wound in his torso. She fell back, staring. Before her eyes, the wound was healing.

At first she thought it was a trick of the uncertain light or her desperate imagination, but all too soon she realized it was real, it was true, it was happening. The fountain of blood slowed, thickened, finally stopped. Torn muscles began to knit, sliced skin formed a pale pink scar that began at the lower end of the cut and gradually traveled upward across his torso, closing the wound with fresh tissue. In another moment even the scar began to fade until, except for the bloodstains on his skin and clothing, there was no evidence of an injury whatsoever.

Gillian brought her shaking fingers to her lips as though to stifle a cry, but no sound came out. She could taste his blood on her fingers. She wanted to scream, she wanted to sob, she wanted to scramble to her feet and run as fast as she could from what she had just seen—what she couldn't deny having seen, no matter how hard she tried—but she couldn't. She couldn't make a sound, couldn't move. She could only sit there, shaking and dragging in choked-off breaths, and stare.

Gabriel's lips were twisted into a dry half smile, but in his eyes was such sorrow as she had never seen in another human being. He said quietly, "And so you see, Gillian, you were right. I am a monster."

She thought, *No.* She tried to say it, but the only sound that escaped her throat was a kind of choked half cry, and even that was so low, so muffled by her desperate rasping gasps for breath, that it was hardly audible.

Somehow she was on her feet, backing away. She couldn't take her eyes off his skin, whole and healed now, as smooth and perfect as a newborn's. His robe was soaked with blood; there was blood on her hands. But he was not bleeding.

He stood on legs that were as strong and perfect as they had been an hour ago. He did not try to approach her; nonetheless she continued to back away. She felt the cold stone wall against her shoulders and she put out a hand to steady herself. Even in the dim light she could see the bloody smear she had left on the wall when she touched it.

Her breath was coming fast, too fast. She concentrated on breathing, on making her breath go in and out, because she was afraid if she stopped concentrating, stopped thinking about it, she would start thinking about other things, and if she did that she might start to scream. And if she started to scream she was afraid she would never stop.

He was alive. He should be dead but he was alive. She had seen with her own eyes the blood that ceased to gush, the wound that knit itself together, the scar that faded from purple-red to newborn pink to nothing at all. She had seen it, yet there was a part of her that refused to see it, or at least to fully comprehend what she had seen. She had seen it . . . but it hadn't happened. It had happened . . . but it meant nothing.

In that way, gradually, she overcame the urge to scream. She remembered to breathe. She remained conscious. The human mind, after all, has very limited facilities for dealing with the impossible. One either ignores the preposterous or accepts it. One either acknowledges the inconceivable with an emotion that is not allowed to go beyond the level of "isn't that interesting?"—or one goes mad. It was that simple.

Gillian's emotions were hovering on that dangerous edge between control and collapse. She was clinging to the world of rationality and order by her fingernails, but she was determined to hold on. She was not going to scream. She was not going to pass out. She was not going to cover her face with her hands and sink to her knees and try to blot it out of her mind, because what she had seen was a miracle, and miracles were things of wonder, not horror.

Yet she was terrified.

"How did you do that?" she asked.

The words came out of her throat, but they didn't really sound like any words she had ever uttered before. They were hoarse and choked and badly enunciated, hardly audible above her shaking, rasping breaths. Yet he heard her. He raised his eyes to her and the pain in them was so immense, so pure, that it penetrated her shock and almost took precedence over it.

"I didn't do anything," he answered, so low that she could not be sure she had heard correctly.

Gillian was trembling from head to toe. Even her blood seemed to be quivering in her veins, her heartbeat more of a spasm than a pulse. She had to press her fingers into the wall to remain upright. She couldn't keep her voice steady, no matter how she tried. "Is that— Is that how you healed me?"

"No." Again quietly, so quietly she could barely hear.

"How did you do that?" she repeated. An edge of hysteria was beginning to creep into her tone, and she fought it with all her might. "How could you possibly do that?"

"I didn't do anything!" he cried.

The sudden outburst was so explosive that Gillian shrank back, but she was already pressed against the wall and could go no farther. His voice was hoarse and ragged and his hands were clenched into tight, impotent fists at his sides. Agony dug its lines into his face and darkened his eyes to the color of a stormy sea at midnight. "God in heaven, don't you under-stand, I can't stop it! I would if I could but...I can't!"

The last two words were harsh and broken, as though the pain of uttering them sliced through his vocal cords. Abruptly he turned from her, pushing his hand through his hair.

Gillian could only stand there, clutching the rock wall with her fingertips, and stare at him. She couldn't speak, she couldn't think, she could hardly feel.

He stood in profile to her, looking over the ledge, and she couldn't see his expression. His tone was low and heavy, roughened with anguish and defeat.

"Don't think I haven't tried," he said. "A thou-sand times, a hundred thousand. The blade, the gun, the poison, the most sophisticated and innovative ways by which the human race has learned to rend its limbs and destroy its bodies and separate the soul from this poor earth. I have met them all at one time or another. It is in my genes, you know. A tiny, mu-tant strand of DNA, something so small, so insig-nificant that until this century you did not even have the instruments in the outside world to see it. Yet it has tormented me, this tiny, insignificant defect, for centuries."

Now he turned to look at her. His expression was haggard, and there was such suffering in his eyes as Gillian had never seen on a living human being. "I have sustained uncounted mortal wounds," he said huskily, "survived a hundred plagues, walked through fire and flood and tasted the earths most noxious poisons...and still I live. I have gone to war, I've plumbed the depths of the oceans, I've stepped off cliffs much higher than this one and into the paths of onrushing trains. There's no disease my body cannot defeat, no wound it can't heal, no dismemberment or disfigurement it can't repair. So you see, it's really quite simple."

And now the smallest hint of a bitter smile twisted his lips. It was a chilling sight. "No matter how much I might sometimes wish it," he said in a flat, almost matter-of-fact tone, "I cannot die. Ever."

Gillian could hear her heart beating now. Slow and heavy, hurting her chest. She could feel her fingertips, the abraded flesh stinging as she unconsciously tightened her grip on the stone wall. She was shaking, still shaking. She wanted to speak, but the words came out only as a whisper.

"No. That's...impossible."

"You have seen it."

"No. It can't be. No one lives forever. It's just not possible."

"Would you like to have another demonstration?" he demanded suddenly, sharply. "Shall I fling myself over the ledge here, so that you can witness the horror again for yourself? Will that please you, Gillian?"

He whirled toward the edge of the ledge, and she screamed, "No!"

He turned with a tempest of rage and pain in his eyes, and Gillian realized then that she had pushed herself away from the wall, one arm extended as though to catch him or draw him back. Gabriel's eyes fell to her arm, and the anger slowly left them. He made a small movement with his hand, as though to reach for hers.

It was pure instinct that caused Gillian to withdraw her hand abruptly, an instinct born of fear and confusion. It startled her as much as it must have hurt him, and she pressed her fingers to her mouth. "No."

And what she was thinking was *Not yet, not now, I can't deal with this now. I can't even think about this now. I'll go mad if I do. Just make it all go away....*

He lifted his eyes to hers, and the sorrow there tore through her heart. He dropped his hand.

Gillian wanted to tell him she was sorry. She wanted to take the moment back when she had withdrawn her hand, she wanted to erase that look from his eyes, she wanted to erase everything that had happened in the entire past hour. She wanted to understand, she wanted to believe, she wanted to help.

What she did was turn and, clinging to the wall, stumbling, sobbing and not looking back, she ran down the stairs.

GILLIAN COULD NOT remember a deeper quiet. She had never noticed before, but since she had come here, there had always been a background current of movement and sound, the ebb and flow of normal life in a thriving culture. Footsteps in the corridor, a distant murmur, a rustle of clothing. Servants moving in and out of her quarters. A muffled giggle. Running water, the subtle hum of whatever machinery made this place work. But now... nothing.

It was as though everything had been turned off, isolating her in her own little corner of this world as effectively as a ship set adrift. Had word of her defection spread so quickly? Had Gabriel given orders to keep her in quarantine? Was she being shunned? Or had rumors spread as rumors will that she had tried to harm the noble Gabriel and the natives were even now plotting their revenge?

Did any of it matter? The elegant, Renaissance-style suite of rooms she had called home since coming here now felt like a tomb. She had never known a deeper silence.

And then she remembered that she had. The night after Jerry's funeral.

She lay on her bed, her eyes swollen and aching from weeping, too exhausted to cry anymore or to even think, but unable to turn off the thoughts. Fragments raced around inside her head, some so inconsequential they slipped out of her consciousness like sand through a sieve, others so lofty, so terrifying in their significance, she could not grasp them for more than a moment. The meaning of life. The certainty of death. The clouds and cherubs on the ceiling above Gabriel's bed. There were no clouds above her bed. Snatches of memory: *Did you want him to live forever? We always want the ones we love to live forever....* An afternoon picnic in a garden. Eyes that blazed with passion, ached with sorrow. Eyes that saw forever....

She muffled a moan and turned on her side, crossing her arms over her stomach as though the pain were a physical one. And in a way it was. Every time she thought of Gabriel, saw his face, remembered his smile, heard his voice, the blow felt like a hammering in the pit of her stomach, a coldness that spread through her veins and left her numb. She didn't want it to be true. *Don't let it be true. Just let everything be the way it was. Make him normal again.*

But nothing had been normal, she was forced to admit, since she had come here. *He* had not been normal. This place was far from normal. The signs had been there all the time, and so many things made sense now.

Gabriel *had* built this place, only he had done so centuries and centuries ago. The construction itself might have *taken* centuries—for a man with no deadlines imposed by the limitations of his own life span, time must be meaningless and any project can be completed, no matter how grand the scale.

And the people here, with their European names and their strange mix of cultures and languages— they had been interacting with Gabriel for generations, not just years. The vast collection of museum-quality treasures this place contained—just the odds and ends Gabriel had picked up over the years. A painting he fancied, a chair that was comfortable, a goblet won in a game of chance.

As for Gabriel himself, his expansive education, the authority with which he spoke on almost every subject, the odd little gaps in his cultural literacy... He had lived through history Gillian could only speculate about. He had witnessed firsthand the truths the books had ignored; he could have *written* the books. Yet what seemed like only a short time to him might have been a score of years or more that he had been hiding away in this cave at the ends of the earth. Naturally a few of the finer points of modern civilization might have eluded him.

*I believe this,* Gillian realized with a kind of dim and distant fascination. *I really believe that this man is a thousand years old or more and will live forever....*

She rolled over on her back again and turned her eyes to the ceiling. What choice did she have, really, except to believe? In the face of such overwhelming evidence, what choice did she really have?

No, it was not the fact that she believed this impossible thing that surprised her so, but the fact that it filled her with such horror. She had seen him fall and her heart had been torn in two. She had knelt beside him and prayed he wouldn't die. She would gladly have given any part of herself to have him whole again . . . and then when her prayer was answered, when he stood before her whole and healed, she had run away from him in terror.

It seemed to Gillian then that she had been running her entire life. She had run from the cutting-edge challenges of her field to the safety of marriage and an anonymous little professorship in an unpretentious university. She had run from the stultifying loneliness of widowhood to this remote corner of the Andes in search of adventure and validation; she had found both and more, and then she had tried to run from that. She had run from Gabriel when she thought he was a criminal, and she had run from him when she discovered he was a living miracle.

Gillian sat up slowly and swung her legs over the side of the bed. Sooner or later she would have to stop running—she had always known that. And now seemed as good a time as any.

"IT WASN'T HER FAULT."

Gabriel was in the library, standing over an open copy of Dante. He had come to help Phillipe catalog the books, for that was an activity he always found innately soothing to the mind. Today he couldn't even concentrate long enough to begin.

He had picked up the Dante, opened it on a reading stand, and there he had stood for the past fifteen minutes or so. He wasn't even reading, merely touching the page, seeing the patterns made by the ink, smelling the musty rich scent of leather and paper. Though he had perfected the most advanced preservation techniques for this library, the aging process had begun on many of the volumes before they came into his hands. The pages of the Dante were brittle and yellowed at the edges, and the leather bindings were beginning to crack. Gabriel stroked the damaged pages lightly, knowing that the oils from his hands were doing even more irreparable harm, but finding it difficult to care. He felt as old and dried out inside as the pages of the book.

"It was my fault, from the beginning," he went on, speaking more to himself than to Phillipe. "I was arrogant, selfish, intent on my own reckless amusement...and, perhaps worst of all, I was so sure I was invulnerable to all those weaknesses. So certain I was in control...but I wasn't, not from the moment I found her. I *should* have outgrown such foolishness, but clearly I haven't. I must take full responsibility for what has happened."

Phillipe carefully rubbed another volume with a specially treated cloth and shelved it. His silence was not condemning or judgmental, merely respectful of his friend's grief.

Gabriel lightly let his fingertips trace the text. "'Abandon all hope, ye who enter here,'" he read, barely above a whisper. He closed the volume quietly, yet stood there for another long moment, staring at it.

"I should have been more careful," Gabriel said, looking up from the book at last. "I should have known better. It seems to me that I must once have known better. Didn't I, Phillipe?"

And then his lips tightened in a faint semblance of his old cynical smile and he said, "But how foolish of me. You couldn't possibly remember that far back. You've known me less than fifty years, after all."

Phillipe shelved another volume. "What will you do?" he asked sensibly.

"I don't know." The heaviness of Gabriel's voice, the slight slump of his shoulders, reflected the enormity of his defeat. But then, when the steadiness of Phillipe's gentle gaze demanded an answer, he said, "She can't stay here any longer, of course." He drew a breath and pronounced the next words as he was turning to leave—symbolically turning his back on the entire matter, finishing it. "Have someone guide her out."

"I don't think we can do that," Phillipe said.

Gabriel snapped his head around with a glare that would have weakened a lesser man. But Phillipe had known too many of his moods, seen him through too much anguish, to be intimidated now.

"First of all," he said, "no one will guide her. The old legends have a strong hold, and the Protectors take their duty seriously. No one may enter unless *you* bring them. No one may leave."

Gabriel's frown darkened. "That is foolishness. You take her if you can't find anyone else."

"Think about that," Phillipe said gently. "Think about *her*. What do you imagine will happen when she returns to her friends, her colleagues, the writers of news in the place where she lives? She is a trained observer and a person of authority. She will tell what she has found—of course she will. Many will scoff— she may lose her credibility in her field, perhaps even her job—but they will listen to her, even if they don't believe. And they will come, looking for this place. Looking for you. The peace we have known for thousands of years will be destroyed. There will be no place you can hide. Is that what you want?"

A flicker of uncertainty crossed Gabriel's eyes. "She won't speak of it," he said brusquely. "She would be foolish to do so."

"Will you trust her to do what is not foolish?" demanded Phillipe with only a trace of impatience. "Was it foolish of her to start up that mountain trail against the advice of her colleagues with only a single servant for help? Was it foolish of her to try to escape this place by climbing thousands of feet into the air on scaffolding that has been on the verge of disintegration for a hundred years? Has she done one thing that was *not* foolish since she came here?"

Gabriel remembered the night she had tottered from her sickbed to search for him, winding through the maze of unfamiliar corridors in what might very well have been a hostile place until she found what she sought. Foolish? Oh, yes. But on that night she had captured his heart, and everything she had done since then, foolish or not, had only tightened the snare.

Gabriel dropped his gaze as the fatigue once again crept across his features. "She has been no more foolish than I," he said. "Once again I give you your due, for you warned me from the beginning. And let this be a lesson to you, my friend—with age does not always come wisdom."

He turned again to leave the room, fully aware that Phillipe's question remained unanswered. He did not know what he was going to do—about Gillian, about himself, about anything. For the first time in too long to remember, he had no answers.

When he rounded the aisle in front of the door, Gillian was standing there.

She was wearing the same dust-streaked clothing in which he had last seen her. Her hair looked as though it had been combed with her fingers, her eyes swollen and her cheeks were still pale. Looking at her took his breath away.

For the longest time he simply stared at her, memorizing her and drinking her in. He hadn't expected to see her again. He had been certain she wouldn't want to see him. Yet she stood there looking at him, and he saw no horror in her eyes, no repulsion.

Gabriel said over his shoulder, a little hoarsely, "Phillipe, leave us, please."

After a moment, Phillipe's footsteps moved softly past on the stone floor. If he even glanced in Gillian's direction as he left, Gabriel did not see it. And neither did Gillian. Her eyes were fixed on Gabriel.

Looking at him almost took her breath away. She had tried to imagine how she would feel when this moment came, when she saw him again, but of all the things she had expected, this sense of wonder, of simple unadulterated awe, was not among them.

He was alive. He was unharmed. He was here, as strong and as beautiful as he had ever been. And seeing him, whole and real and close enough to touch, sent a wave of joyous amazement through her that left her weak.

He had changed his clothes, from the white open robe he usually wore to one of plain brown, closed up the front, like those favored by Phillipe and some of the older men. His hair was tied back severely, and the sleeves of the garment almost covered his hands. It was a stark, almost clerical look, emphasized by the lines of weariness in his face, the cautious shadows that shielded his eyes.

He didn't speak, and for a long time Gillian could not make her voice work, either. She couldn't even remember the words she wanted to say, if she had ever known what they were at all. But when Phillipe's footsteps had faded away and they were completely alone, she knew she couldn't simply stand there forever. She took a step farther into the room.

She pressed her palms together to steady her voice. "I have some things to say. Then I have some questions—a lot of questions. I know I have no right to ask, and I don't deserve anything more from you, but I'd appreciate it if you would just listen. You don't have to answer my questions if you don't want to."

He didn't answer. He simply stood there, watching her, waiting for her to go on. His expression was indiscernible.

Gillian found she couldn't meet his eyes, not right away. She half turned from him, fixing her gaze on a shelf of medical texts. There were hundreds of them.

"I should have known I would find you here," she said softly. "I looked everywhere, but this room has always seemed to be where you belong."

She turned around and forced herself to look at him. "I haven't been a very good friend," she said simply.

Her hands were still clenched tightly together, though not from fear or anxiety—at least, not in the ordinary sense. The only thing she feared now was that she would say the wrong thing and he would reject her.

"You saved my life," she went on. "You brought me here, you offered me every hospitality, you never did anything to offend or threaten me. You were kind and entertaining and—for the most part, anyway— patient. I repaid you with suspicion and disbelief. On the flimsiest of evidence I was ready to believe you were a common criminal. I—" And here she dropped her eyes to her hands and had to clear her throat before she could go on. "There were a lot of crazy, mixed-up reasons I acted the way I did, and I suppose you know most of them. But the bottom line is—I wasn't a very good friend, and I'm ashamed of myself."

Now she raised her eyes to his again, clenching her hands until they hurt. "I'm sorry," she said.

After what seemed a very long time, Gabriel's lips curved upward very slightly in a smile. It was not a bitter expression or a mocking one, and it even held a hint of its former gentle charm. Mostly, the smile was sad.

"And so, Gillian," he said, "at last you believe what you see with your own eyes."

It wasn't much in the way of acknowledgment or forgiveness, but relief swept through Gillian. She took a hesitant step toward him.

"I always wanted to believe in you, Gabriel," she said. "I was just...afraid."

Something quick and unexpected flickered across his eyes—hope or passion or a touch of fire—and was just as quickly subdued. A new caution, vaguely laced with hope, was in his expression as he said, "And you are afraid no longer?"

She continued toward him. "Should I be?"

His jaw hardened. "You have uncovered a monster."

"No," she replied, holding his gaze. "I've discovered an angel. And that's what you've always been to me."

She stopped about two feet before him and extended her hands. She could feel her heart pounding, filling up the space between them. He dropped his gaze to her hands and looked at them for what seemed like forever. Then, slowly, he extended his own hands and closed his fingers over hers.

Gillian took one more breathless step, and was in his arms.

## Chapter Ten

Gillian sank into his kiss, into the taste and power of
him, the surge of strength and engulfing sweetness.
And she was lost. His touch filled her veins with heat
and effervescence and her mind with colors. She was
drawn into him as effortlessly as metal to a magnet,
and magic sang between them. She had always
known his power, but now she understood it. The
awe she once felt had become simple wonder. She
was afraid...and she wasn't.

His hands were hard on her scalp, holding her
close, drinking her in. And then his fingers tightened fractionally, as though he were fighting his own
instincts, and he dragged his mouth away.

"Don't do this, Gillian," he murmured, breathing hard. "I won't let you do this."

Gillian lifted her hands to his face. His skin was
flushed and damp, his eyes brilliant with desire.
"You said the time was mine to choose, Gabriel,"
she whispered. "I was so foolish, so small-minded

and afraid...but when I thought I had lost you, everything changed and I saw what I had wasted...."

His eyes flared with intensity, and she could see the long tendons in his neck tighten. "You don't know what you're saying. You're reacting to the shock of what you've seen, and in a moment you'll regret having come to me—"

She shook her head. "The only things I've ever regretted in my life are those I haven't done."

He searched her face, and she saw far back in his eyes a flickering of hope, the desperate need to believe what she said even as he guarded himself from hurt and disappointment. "You know what I am."

She said softly, "We always want the ones we love to live forever, Gabriel."

She felt his deep inhalation of breath and saw the exquisite tenderness that came over his face. Slowly he lowered his forehead to hers, hiding his expression from her. His voice was husky. "I never wanted to care for you.... I can't care for you."

Gillian's hands slipped down to his neck, caressing it, and she closed her eyes against the pain she felt from him. "Don't push me away, Gabriel," she whispered. "I know how it is for you.... I know what it's like to be afraid to live because you know you're only going to lose the ones you love, the things you care about. I've been like that since Jerry died. But now...everything about me has changed since I came here. It's as though—" Here she had to stop, struggling for the right words. Her fingers slipped beneath the heavy fall of his hair, cradling his head. "It's as though I really died during the landslide and was born again. I want to believe in the impossible now, I want to take chances. I'm ready to risk loving again, all because of you."

He lifted his head, his eyes dark and sober. "Gillian," he said, "don't let it mean more than it must."

"It's too late," she said softly. "It already does."

Once again they came together with the inevitability of the tide flowing to shore. His mouth covered hers, and she was engulfed in his embrace. Heat flared and senses whirled, thunder pounded through her veins. She was weak with need, strong with certainty. She had never been more sure of anything in her life than she was of this man, and she had never been more afraid.

When he swept her off her feet and into his arms, she closed her eyes and let him take her where he would.

Gabriel could not recall the last time he had surrendered control so completely—uncounted aeons ago, if ever. He knew with all his heart and mind that only disaster could come of this, that pain and loss was the inevitable result of loving her. Yet it was as he had told Phillipe: from the moment he had seen her, from the first instant, reason had fled and he had lost control.

He told himself he was prepared for losing her. He had been prepared from the beginning, and the look of horror and repugnance that had filled her face on the ledge had only made it easier. Yet, she had come to him. She had come to him and his heart began to sing, and until she stood before him and looked at him without fear, he had never allowed himself to admit how very much he wanted to see her look at him like that. How much he had wanted her to come to him.

She touched him and his blood was on fire. She caressed him and his soul quaked with joy. And when he looked into her eyes and saw the tenderness there, the acceptance and the need, no power on earth could have stopped him from drawing her close, from sweeping her into his arms and carrying her to his bed.

He had lived the lives of a thousand men and loved a thousand women, but none of them had been real before Gillian. That small and basic physical act he had once found so easy to ignore now seemed the single most important consequence in the world, the reason for man's creation, the driving force of his existence. To love this woman, to make love to her, to claim her, to pleasure her, to know her. To become part of her, to take a part of her into himself. How could he have lived so long without her? How could his thirsting, aching soul endure another moment alone?

And so it was that, though all his senses shouted warnings to him, though reason promised nothing but pain for his foolishness, he knew nothing but the swelling need that filled his heart, the fire of passion that consumed his body. He moved through the secret corridors and private rooms without seeming to move at all. He reached his sleeping chamber, his private place, the bed no woman had shared before. He settled Gillian among the furs and tasted her inside his mouth, felt the silken fall of her hair against his arm and the caress of her hands reaching for him as he drew away from her.

He cast aside his garments in a single careless motion and felt the whisper of cool air on his naked skin. He was fevered and strong, powerful in his need and weak in his longing. He was aware of a hundred—a thousand—sensations, and all of them felt new to him. The aching, almost unbearable fullness of his loins. The rushing of his heartbeat and the pounding of blood in his veins, the stinging of his skin as pores opened up to new sensations, the tightening of his muscles, the expansion of his lungs, needing her, needing her.

He was a barbarian in a fur skin savoring the victorious moment of conquest. He was a priest humbled in the presence of a goddess. He was a poet in the throes of inspiration, a hunter intoxicated by the chase, he was filled with savage power and primal need. He was lover, husband, guardian. He was a man in love with a woman, made strong by her, made weak by her, and when she opened her arms to him he sank helplessly, hungrily into the wonder that was her.

"Gabriel..." she whispered, and her breath caressed his ear, sending electric shivers down his spine. "Angel..."

Her hands caressed his back, sliding down to his buttocks and tightening there as she arched against him urgently. He suppressed a groan against her neck, gathering her close. He wanted to drown in her. He almost felt as though holding her, wrapped around her just like that, was all he could ever want for all his uncounted days. Just to hold her, just to taste her, just to capture this exquisite moment of desire so sharp and sweet it was almost too intense to bear... It was enough. It was all he could ask.

And yet it wasn't. For her urgency only spoke to him of the shortness of their time together and the need to make it last, and he whispered, "No, my love. Let me show you...."

He caught her arms, drawing them forward, kissing each inch of flesh that was exposed, as the fullness of her sleeves fell away. Ah, the taste of her. He let it seep into his skin, flow into his veins, bury itself deep inside his memory, to be guarded and treasured through the long barren years ahead. He drank her in, her small-boned wrists, the tender flesh at the crook of her arm, the curve of her collarbone. He felt her shudder with desire. He covered her mouth with his and took her breath into his lungs. He filled himself with her, grew dizzy from the power of her.

She was wearing one of those strange modern skirts she favored, and when he tugged at the waistband, the fasteners came apart in his hand. He stripped the garment from her and felt her strong, slender legs entwining with his, the softness of her belly pressing against his hardness. He tore his mouth from hers, breathing hard.

Through the heated haze of his own passion, her face came into focus beneath him, lovely, adored. Her eyes were dark and brilliant, her face soft with the flush of need, her dark hair tumbled across his pillow like ripples of glistening chocolate. Just looking at her filled him with a new surge of sensation, of wonder and desire.

He cupped her face with his hands, caressing every curve and plane. He murmured her name, and even the sound of it was beautiful to him. He opened her shirt, again with a soft tearing sound, for his clumsy fingers knew nothing of buttons or of patience. Her breasts were soft globes tipped with pink, distinctly outlined by the tanned skin that was exposed by her summer garments. With his hands he cupped her breasts, tightening his fingers gently. He saw the pleasure smooth out the lines in her face, darkening her eyes another fraction, and his heart began to pound strong and hard. This intimacy, this knowing of Gillian in all her secret, private parts, the giving and sharing—this was what he craved. This was all that mattered of life. This was worth any cost, just to know her, to adore her, for however small a moment.

Gillian lifted her arms, loosening the thong that bound back his hair and combed her fingers through it, drawing it forward like a veil that enshrouded the two of them, sealed in their mingled scents and body heat. Gabriel covered one firm, upthrust breast with his mouth, tasting its sweetness. He felt the tensing of pleasure that rippled through her muscles and heard her muffled moan. Her knee came up to caress his naked hip, holding him tightly against her, and a new surge of desire peaked within him.

Gabriel wound his legs around hers and, cupping her buttocks with his hands, rolled over on his side with her, drawing her into the curve of his body. "Ah, beloved," he whispered, kissing her face, her neck, her eyes. "Someday soon I will show you the secrets of lovers throughout the ages, I will teach your body pleasures you have never imagined before. But for now—" he gathered a double handful of her hair and brought it to his face, inhaling the scent, luxuriating in the texture "—just let me love you."

"Gabriel . . . yes. Please . . ."

The luxury of her kiss on his neck, the press of her teeth and the hungry, demanding strokes of her hands, sent new arrows of yearning through him, spiraling waves of heat and need. He slipped his hand between their bodies and into the warm, secret nest between her thighs. He watched her eyes as his fingertips caressed and opened the silky moist flesh, penetrating slowly and then withdrawing, preparing her body to receive him. The urgency of need on her face tightened, and she pressed against him, finger-nails digging into the muscled flesh of his shoulders, suppressing a cry of need in the curve of his neck.

Gabriel's breath was thundering through his lungs, his heartbeat an anvil in his chest. He was helpless against the depth of his need for this woman, com-pletely mastered by her, yet never had he been stronger, more empowered, more alive. He had wanted so many things for this their first union, he had planned it so carefully in his mind. But the re-ality of her swept away all his dreams and all his rea-son, leaving only instinct, overwhelming and primitive, carnal and strong.

His mouth sought hers, and he fitted her hips against his. Her knees pressed into his waist as he poised himself against her, savoring the soft, tender, welcoming heat that beckoned him. Though he wanted to go slowly, restraint eluded him and he felt himself drawn helplessly inside. Gillian gasped at the first strong pressure of his entry, and he could not know whether it was from pleasure or pain. He caught her face between his hands and murmured something to her—he knew not what.

The passion they had created flared beyond the control of either of them. With a cry, she lifted her-self to him and he thrust deep inside her, buried within her, lost to the dark rich heat of infinity. Her open mouth caressed his face, quick hot breaths flooded his skin. He tasted perspiration and musk and the sweet wild essence that was Gillian. Her fingers tangled in his hair, tugging at it. His fingers pressed into her waist, the delicate framework of her ribs, following the curve of her spine and molding her buttocks. Their movements fell into a sharp, urgent synchronized rhythm as she thrust against him and he drove into her, seeking and grasping, knowing what they sought was theirs to take whenever they wished it.

Again and again he took her to the very edge of the abyss and then poised there, aching, bursting, prolonging the pleasure as though this might be their last chance to ever know it. When she wept with need, when her muscles trembled and her breath grew ragged and she writhed against him, he took her over the edge.

How simple a thing it was to put aside his own pleasure and focus on hers, how necessary, how inevitable. He wanted to give her everything, to be everything for her, for only in her fulfillment was he alive. Only in her arms did he feel human.

She tossed her head on the pillow, grasping for him, and he felt her body begin to convulse around him. He caught her close to him, and though she cried out in protest, he rolled under her so that she was astride him. A canopy of stars and angels and Gillian's face blurred and swirled before his eyes. She sobbed with need, clinging to him, and he was bursting, body and soul. He took her waist and urged her to sit up, watching her eyes as she took even more of him inside her. He entwined his fingers with hers and held her hands tightly as he thrust deep into her, pressing against the very heart of her womb. He heard her cry out and he released himself to the sensation as the rapture overtook them both.

She collapsed against him and he rose to meet her, enfolding her in his arms, tasting her, breathing her, absorbing her as wave after wave of powerful, wringing pleasure drained through them. He spilled himself inside her and it felt as though he relinquished his soul. Yet he took a part of her into himself, the essence of her that could never be extracted again because it was blended into his mind, his heart, his very blood.

Gillian, before whom he had never known the meaning of living. Without whom he would never be completely alive again.

## Chapter Eleven

They slept. Or at least Gillian slept, and she dreamed of times of old, of noble knights and ladies fair, of coliseums and olive groves, and as she lay curled inside the circle of Gabriel's embrace it was almost as though she shared his dreams. She opened her eyes to the parting of the heavens, cerulean blue and starry nights and cherubs among the clouds. And Gabriel's eyes, bluer than any blue devised by man or nature, met hers.

The muscles in her legs and back were strained and tired, and she ached faintly at the place where their two bodies were joined; for a moment it was as though she could still feel him inside her, and it was a wonderful feeling. Her skin was sticky with the residue of his perspiration and hers, even a little raw in places from the roughness of his beard shadow. She felt washed through, renewed, worn-out and reborn. Her body did not even feel like hers anymore.

He was there, holding her, looking at her. His hair was loose and still damp in places, falling forward over one shoulder. Her eyes rested on the curve of his collarbone, and that sight alone filled her with wonder. Strong, real. The masculine shoulder, the swell of pectoral muscle, the column of neck. Holding her, loving her. She looked at him and she felt a sudden shyness that bordered on awe.

He lifted her hand and smoothed a strand of hair from her cheek. "Gillian," he said softly. "Are you all right? You slept so long."

Her shyness melted away in the face of his concern. She lifted a hand to his shoulder, stroking the fall of his hair with the back of her knuckles. "Did I?"

"I didn't mean to be so forceful. Tell me if I hurt you."

She smiled. "You made me feel— No, I won't tell you. It will only make you vain. Or are you above that sort of thing?"

For the first time his expression relaxed, and a teasing smile came into his eyes. "No man ever outgrows appreciation for compliments on his sexual prowess. I will enjoy any you care to give me."

Gillian lifted her arms to his neck, amusement fading to a tenderness so intense it formed a lump in her throat. "You make me feel like I've never felt before,'' she said huskily. "You make me feel...more than myself.''

His eyelids lowered, shielding his expression. He caught one of her hands and brought it to his lips, kissing the fingers gently. "And you, Gillian,'' he said simply, "make me feel human. It has been too long since I could say that.''

Love and longing welled up inside her, a feeling so vast and all-encompassing it left her weak. For a moment she couldn't even speak, and when the words came out they were not the ones she wanted to say. The question was born of need and necessity, an answer she did not want to hear, a question she could not ignore.

"Oh, Gabriel,'' she whispered, searching his face, "what will become of us?''

He kissed her fingers again, and then he raised his eyes to hers. There was no surprise in his face, but the sadness and acceptance was unmistakable. "The only thing that can. I will love you as long as you will let me. You'll grow tired of me—''

"I'll never grow tired of you.''

His eyes were kind and understanding—and filled with sorrow. "Then,'' he answered gently, returning her hand to the pillow on which it once had rested, "you'll simply grow old.''

His words chilled her, and Gillian did not know what to say. He sat up, leaning back against the ornately carved headboard, beautiful and unselfconscious in his nakedness. Her heart ached for him, for them, for all that should have been theirs and all they could never have.

Gillian lifted herself to one elbow beside him, lightly placing a hand on his thigh. "When did you first know?" she asked softly.

He glanced at her, then away. After a moment he began to speak, his tone abstracted yet matter-of-fact. "I was a sailor, in a time long before written history. I fell from the mast in a storm. I should have died...but I didn't. I watched my mother, my father, my wife, my brothers age and die...and I lived on. I went to war and fell, pierced through the heart by a sword...and got up to fight again.

"Though much of it is a blur as I look back, I cannot be proud of the man I was then. In those early years I was wild in my power and terrified of it. I abused it and denied it and, I think, more than once, succumbed to madness because of it. At last, in despair, I grew resigned. I went again to sea, crossed jungles, climbed mountains.

"Ah, Gillian, I discovered more about this planet on which we live in my first two hundred years upon it than is known even today by the brightest of your scientists. And when I was tired, weary unto death with knowing and seeing and learning and losing, with trying and failing and trying again...then I came to this place, which was old even then and as lost as I was. Here I began to make my home, and as the centuries rolled past, it was here I have always returned, when the miseries and ugliness of the world of which I have seen too much begin to press down on me. I'm safe here.''

Gillian was silent for a time, struggling with the enormity of what life must have been like for him, trying to comprehend the miracle of this man who lay beside her. He had lived a thousand lifetimes. He had seen nations rise and fall, civilizations flourish and disappear. He had walked with kings, taken counsel from the wisdom of the ages. He had sat at the feet of ancient philosophers and danced in the ballrooms of Vienna and fought a hundred wars. He had known queens and enchantresses and history's most powerful courtesans. And he loved *her.*

She raised her eyes to the profile of his face. ''Does anyone else know?''

''Some have, over the years. Phillipe knows, and his father before him. They were my great friends. Others have chosen to come back here with me and keep my secret. It is to them that you may credit the children with European features for, to answer your question—'' a hint of wry reproval came into his tone. ''—I have no offspring. My genetic deformity, as is very often the case among mutants, has left me sterile.''

Gillian felt a miserable heat stain her cheeks. "You're not a mutant," she said.

He shrugged. "A matter of semantics."

Gillian let her eyes travel over his body, from the strong sharp jaw and the silky hair, across the breadth of shoulders and chest, to the strength of thighs and the dark intimacy of his sex. What she saw was man perfected, maleness incarnate, humanity at its most noble. Renewed desire swelled within her from simply looking at him, and her fingers tightened on his thigh without volition. He looked down at her and smiled, reading her emotions, knowing her mind. He covered her hand with his, and wonder surged through her with his touch.

"You are not a mutant," she repeated softly. Then she said, "What do you know about your condition?"

"Nothing that can be condensed into a few moments of pillow talk." But when he saw her expression, the teasing left his eyes and he replied, "It seems to be linked to a shifting-antigen virus that's carried in my blood. I've been able to narrow it down as to form and type, but the connection is still obscure."

She frowned. "But how can a virus, or even a component of the blood, affect DNA?"

"I didn't claim it was a common affliction."

A cautious excitement stirred within Gillian, and she sat up a little straighter. "But if it's a virus, there must be a cure."

His expression was tolerant. "Must there? Even I have only been able to isolate and create antigens for a small percentage of the viruses known to afflict the human body, and there are hundreds—perhaps thousands—yet to be discovered."

Her excitement grew. "But it's *possible*. New discoveries are being made every day, laboratories around the world are filled with researchers day and night. For God's sake, Gabriel, why don't you go to them? Let them study you. Let them help!"

"That," he replied with a kind of weary patience, "is exactly what I have spent a good many years trying to avoid. I am not a laboratory animal, Gillian. Neither do I have any supernatural powers to enable me to escape from the clutches of those who would 'study' me, whether their intentions be for good or ill. Would you condemn me to a four-square room with bars on the window for all eternity? For that, I assure you, is exactly what would happen if I were to go to anyone else for help."

She was on her knees now, the covers falling away as she wrapped her hands around his arm. "It doesn't have to be like that, Gabriel," she said, though she had to fight back uncertainty. "You haven't been outside this place in a long time. You don't know the kind of technology that exists today...."

The look he gave her was sympathetic. "Gillian," he said gently, "you have seen what I've created here. You've seen my laboratory. Do you seriously think anything your world of science has to offer will surprise or impress me? And can you honestly believe they could discover anything in their frail handful of years that I haven't already learned after centuries of study?"

Her head was whirling with half-formed thoughts and barely dared ideas, questions and possibilities flickering across the screen of her mind at lightning pace, far too fast for her to grasp. Had she only this morning awakened an ordinary woman with common needs and petty grievances? But a miracle had opened her eyes and love had transformed her and nothing would ever be the same again.

*It shouldn't be like this,* she thought with a touch of despair. After the love they had just made, they should be lying in each other's arms, reliving every moment, speaking of poetry and eternity and all the wonders that lovers do. They should be celebrating the magic they had made together, exploring new delights, making promises, making plans. Instead they spoke of science and impossibilities and cold, hard facts.

She was in love with this man, this king of time, this guardian of the ages. His body had merged with hers, his soul had touched her own. Could any woman experience such a thing and remain unchanged? Could she pretend his pains were not her own, his needs were of no concern, his suffering did not affect her? And yet she could not forget who she was and where she had come from; she could not ignore the woman she had been when she awoke that morning. And she had questions that needed answers, responsibilities to the world she had left behind that still tugged at her.

She struggled to put her thoughts, random and inchoate as they were, into words. "I— Gabriel, please tell me." She drew a steadying breath. "When I was injured so badly...it wasn't amnesia or my imagination, was it? You really did treat me, and I really did recover in only four days?"

He hesitated, but only for a moment, as though coming to the decision that nothing he could do or say could possibly do any more harm. He withdrew his arm and got out of bed, walking with a liquid economy of movement across the room, where he donned a robe—rich blue this time—and belted it. "There's no need for the clumsy risks the surgeons of your outside world take, Gillian," he answered. "I couldn't let you suffer that way."

Gillian could hardly form the question, and in the end she supplemented the two words with a helpless gesture of her wrist. "But . . . how?"

Again he smiled. He stood with one shoulder resting against a carved armoire, and his posture appeared relaxed. But Gillian could see the tension in his neck, his shoulders, in the way he held his head.

"Put yourself in my place," he said. "If you had an incurable physical condition and endless time and resources at your disposal, how would you spend your life? I have become something of an expert on the human body and its various ailments. I have spent centuries studying and practicing medicine in all its many forms. I've sought the wisdom and perfected the techniques of practitioners long since forgotten by your modern world, and I've developed techniques of my own. I have no magic in my fingers, Gillian," he said seriously, "merely a sum of knowledge and experience that death has never diluted. And I used that to make you whole again, that is all."

And slowly it all began to come together for her, like a kaleidoscope of broken glass that suddenly, unexpectedly formed a pattern of breathtaking brilliance. All of the accumulated wisdom of humanity's history was at this man's fingertips. He had forgotten nothing, lost nothing, left no avenue unexplored. What quantum leaps in knowledge might have been reached had not the achievements of Einstein and Pasteur and da Vinci been interrupted by death? Would the world ever know how many breakthroughs in science, medicine and the arts had been lost forever because the men who might have made them had simply run out of time?

But Gabriel knew. Gabriel had never run out of time, had never been distracted, had never been forced to abandon an idea or delay a project. The technology she had seen here was only the tip of the iceberg. Major surgery performed as easily as slicing bread. Massive injuries healed in a matter of days. His laboratory, the vials and vials of extracts she had mistaken for illegal drugs...

"My God," she said, a little breathlessly. "You must be as far ahead of us as we are to—to the chimpanzee!"

He neither confirmed nor denied, merely looked at her, waiting, it seemed, for the inevitable.

Gillian suddenly felt uncomfortable, sitting naked in his bed while he stood fully clothed. She reached among the tousled furs and tangled sheets for her shirt and pulled it on. Gabriel watched her with an odd, rather poignant smile, and Gillian was as aware as he was of the symbolism of the gesture. Of all the things that separated them, clothing seemed to be the least important.

She clutched the shirt with its missing buttons over her breasts, her mind racing, thoughts and hopes and frantic half-formed plans tumbling over one another inside her head. *What will become of us?* she had asked. Had she really wanted to know the answer to that question? Had she imagined there even was one?

"Come with me, Gabriel," she blurted out in sudden desperation. "Leave this place. See what the outside world is like now. Come home with me."

His expression gentled. He came to sit beside her, laying one hand against her face, stroking it gently. The yearning and regret in his eyes was so exquisite, so tender, it broke her heart. "Don't you think that, above all things, is what I want, Gillian? To go to your quiet little town with its elm trees and its moving-picture show, to sit on your front porch at night and listen to the sounds of normal people living their oh-so-normal lives. But I am not normal, Gillian. There's no place for me in your world."

She knew he was right. She tried to picture him attending faculty parties and playing tennis, but the mind balked. Still she insisted, "You've done it before. You can use makeup to simulate the aging process—"

"For a time," he agreed. "And perhaps I would fool your very clever friends and fellow scientists. Perhaps I would not. And how long, I wonder, my dear, beloved girl, after you began to age and I did not, could you keep my horrible secret?"

Gillian withdrew from his touch, chilled. "I would never betray you," she said hoarsely.

He shook his head gently. "It's not betrayal, my love. It's human nature. You want to help, you want your scientists to help, but in the end nothing can help. Our life together would be barren and tormented, and I can't do that to you—or to myself."

Before he even finished, she was shaking her head adamantly. "How can you say that? For God's sake, Gabriel, you can do your research outside as well as you can here! And think what you could offer the world! Why, as a doctor alone—"

His face suddenly went cold. "No."

He stood and walked away, and his absence—the absence of his warmth, his smile, the light in his eyes—was like a draft of graveyard air blowing across her skin. Gillian got out of bed, hugging her arms across her chest to warm herself. She took a few steps toward him, but he remained standing with his back to her.

"Why not?" she insisted, hating herself for doing so, wishing she could just let it go, wishing she could draw him back into their warm bed of furs and find heaven again. Wishing life could be easy, love could be simple. . . .

Her fists tightened beneath her crossed arms, and she said tightly, "I spent most of my adult life watching a man I cared for very much struggle to save lives, to ease suffering—and then lose that battle himself. You could have saved those lives, Gabriel. You could have eased their suffering. How can you be so selfish?"

"I have nothing to do with the world," he replied stiffly, "and it has nothing to do with me."

"How can you say that?" she cried. "How can you know how to cure half the world's ills and keep those cures buried here with you inside this mountain? How can you live with yourself and do that?"

He remained silent, his shoulders square, his back straight.

Gillian took a deep, somewhat unsteady breath, trying to understand, trying to rationalize . . . and finding it increasingly difficult to do so. "All right," she said in a moment, quietly. "All right, think about this. That component in your blood—did you ever think that *it* might hold the answer to questions scientists have been trying to answer for hundreds of years? We can clone genes now, you know. Do you really have the right to keep this to yourself when by sharing it you might save thousands of lives?"

"For what?" He turned on her, his expression explosive. "This living hell? Do you think I would wish this curse on any other living being?"

His muscles were tense, the veins in his neck prominent. He ran a hand through his hair tightly, and his voice had a hoarse, ragged edge to it. "Do you know what it's like to watch the ones you love grow old and die, one by one—and not just mother, father, wife, friends of one lifetime, but of a dozen, a hundred, over and over again. To suffer such pain of flesh and agony of spirit that you weep for death, knowing it can never come?"

He drew a sharp breath and the struggle with his own anger and frustration was visible. In the end it was simple inevitability, rather than control, that won out.

The tension drained from his shoulders and left defeat. His voice dropped and his eyes seemed old and faraway. "To simply grow tired," he said, "so very tired.... Wars have come and gone, heroes and leaders and bringers of peace, the earth has rent itself in two, mountains have toppled, man has spread his wings into the very ether of outer space...and nothing surprises me anymore, nothing pleases or displeases me." The words were heavy, as though it cost him enormous energy to speak them. "I simply endure."

And then he looked at her. "Until there was you. You have made me want again, need again, care again. I didn't realize how much until today when I almost lost you. Ah, Gillian, what I wouldn't give to be a normal man. To live my life and bear my pains and solve my problems and to love, freely and wholly. To hold in my arms a son of my loins and yours. To build what I can and leave behind what I will, and to rest, when my allotted time was up. I've spent centuries trying to find a way to be nothing more than normal and had finally resigned myself to the impossibility. But you came and made me want again. Made me wish I would be nothing more than a man, loving you."

Gillian felt a single tear escape her flooded eyes and trickle down her cheek. The ache she felt inside was his pain, the emptiness and yearning of a thousand years that he had kept locked inside. But the helplessness and the shame she felt were her own, for how could she presume to judge this man? How could she know what he had witnessed and endured and reached for and lost? How could she demand more of him when already he had given her more than any mortal man had a right to expect? To love her, to let her love him... It was enough. It had to be.

"I don't want to lose you, Gabriel."

He looked at her sadly. "I can't leave this place, Gillian. I can't live in your world. And you won't stay here."

Gillian dashed at another tear, drawing a muffled breath. "Ask me," she whispered.

Surprise darkened his eyes, and cautious disbelief. "Gillian." The word was spoken softly, with hesitance and uncertainly. "You cannot mean that. You have a home outside this place, a career, a place in the world. You can't mean to give all that up."

"I'm not giving up anything," she said, and without thinking it another minute, she knew she spoke the clearest truth she had ever known. "None of that is important. I only have one lifetime, Gabriel. It's not enough—but I want to spend it with you. Please." She extended her hand to him. "Let me."

Gabriel stepped forward and closed his hand around hers. Together they sank back onto the bed, losing themselves in the promise of each other's arms.

## Chapter Twelve

It should have been so simple. Years should have passed in bliss and safety, the two of them working side by side, learning about each other, loving each other, growing rich in the wonder of each other. And in Gillian's dreams it did happen so, a future spinning out in warm pastel colors, a tapestry woven from the brilliant threads of the love she and Gabriel made.... When she awoke, she was alone.

There was a moment of absolute panic, when she thought it had all been a dream from the beginning, that she had never left her safe, cozy home for adventure in the Andes, never met Gabriel, never known the miracle. But gradually the room came into focus—the sky above, the enormous bed cradling her—and gradually her runaway heartbeat slowed. But still she was alone.

She slid out of bed, combing back her hair with her fingers, and pulled on one of his white robes. The garment was as soft as silk and big enough to engulf her two or three times, and it smelled of him. She spent one irresistible moment with her eyes closed, a fold of the material pressed to her face, inhaling his scent. The longing that swelled in her was sharp and poignant; missing him was a physical thing. Wrapping the robe around her and gathering up handfuls at the knee to clear the hem off the floor, she went in search of Gabriel.

She knew there was no need to read anything ominous into his absence; she knew there was a perfectly reasonable explanation for his not being there when she awoke. She did not expect him to be by her side twenty-four hours a day. Nonetheless her heart did not resume its normal rhythm until she heard a sound from the stone chamber to her right and knew, because the remainder of the corridor was so perfectly quiet, that it must be him.

She stood on the threshold of what she recognized immediately as the steam baths. Phillipe had shown them to her one day and invited her to use them anytime, but that was before she felt comfortable enough to do so. It was a mystical, inviting place, with three separate sunken pools surrounded by bromeliad and ferns, swathed in foggy clouds of steam. The bubbling of the hot springs was a musical background, but the splash she had heard came from the central, largest pool. There Gabriel reclined on the natural rock bench that protruded from the pool, his head and shoulders visible above the surface, the remainder of his naked body a wavering form beneath the water. She simply stood there for a moment, filled with wonder for this man she had only begun to know and love.

"Shall I tell you something that will shock you?"

His voice startled her; she hadn't known he was aware of her presence. She stepped into the room. "What?"

"Before you came, I hardly ever wore clothes. It seemed too much of a bother."

She laughed softly. It was a good clean feeling that came from her heart. "You are pagan."

"I have been," he agreed amiably. He lifted one hand to her, wet and steamy. "Will you join me?"

She knelt on the side of the pool, the folds of his oversize robe draping around her. "Is it hot?"

"Very. I had forgotten how stimulating the sensation could be. It's been many years since I took the baths. I think I must have once been quite a sensualist... and you have awakened me to that again."

Gillian gasped as his fingertip, hot and slick, parted her robe and traced a line between her breasts, down the center of her torso, to her navel.

He said huskily, "Come here, Gillian."

He pushed the robe off her shoulders and fastened his hands around her waist. Bracing her hands against his shoulders, Gillian slid into the water.

It was hot. It crept up her body like a fever, slick and steamy and buoyant with minerals. Currents and eddies whirled around her ankles, engulfed her calves, caressed between her legs. Gabriel pulled her close to him, holding her weightless in the water, and her legs encircled his waist. He opened his mouth against hers; she tasted him with slow, deliberate luxury.

"You have brought me life, Gillian," he murmured against her mouth. "If nothing else comes of this, if I should lose you tomorrow, what you have given me already is more than I ever expected. More than I had any right to ask."

"Don't talk like that," she whispered, and tried to turn her face away.

His mouth captured hers again. "You're right," he said at length. "I'm foolish to talk at all when there is so much to simply feel."

He stepped down a few inches and the water lapped at her buttocks, tickling the sensitive nerves of her inner thighs. She gasped at the sensation and a deep light of pleasure came into his eyes as he watched her.

"Like this," he said, and liqu
around her, opening her pores, pe  ding,
cell. "And this...."

He slipped his hands beneath her butt
her slide down his body. Her heart was ding,
slow and heavy. She drew long, deep breaths of
cleansing, dizzying steam. His eyes, his beautiful
face, filled her vision. She could feel the fullness of
him pressed against the center of her. The heat of the
water seemed to be an extension of his heat, engulfing her, filling her.

He let the weight of her body and the movement
of the water ease him into her, until the sensation was
so intense that she wanted to cry out from the pleasure of it, to release herself to its explosive power.
But she stayed still, holding her breath and watching Gabriel's eyes, for that was the greatest pleasure
of all.

"Remember this, Gillian," he whispered. "Remember this moment, this feeling we share. Hold it
deep in your heart, safe from all who would steal it
from you, and know that I will do the same...
forever."

His mouth closed over hers, and he clasped her to
him, holding himself deep inside her until, in a single inevitable rush, the explosion shook them both,
gripping their bodies with a sweet, powerful intensity that sealed them together like forms in molten

ava, like iron in a forge. It was that simple, and that true.

Gabriel cradled her in his arms on the bench. Her hair was wet, and so was was his, as were their faces. She could not remember how they had gotten that way. He stroked her hair. "Shall we get out?"

She shook her head against his chest. "Let's just stay here. Hold me."

He kissed her forehead, smiling gently. "Do you know how long it's been since you first came to my bed?"

Again she shook her head, letting her eyes drift closed.

"Almost forty-eight hours. You've had very little sleep since then."

She lifted her eyes to him, lazily surprised. "Your endurance is remarkable."

He chuckled and kissed her on the lips. "I do love you, Gillian Aldair."

And then the laughter faded from his eyes, but she was too content, too drowsy and in love and sure it would last forever, to wonder why. He shifted her weight in his arms and sat on the bench, holding her. They stayed that way for a long time.

Then Gillian said quietly, "It happened to you before, didn't it? You let them study you, on the outside."

There was the briefest hesitation. "I didn't precisely *let* them. Let's just say I chose my friends—and my time—unwisely. It was in Germany, during a particularly unpleasant episode of their history."

Gillian squeezed her eyes tightly closed, curling her fist against his chest. "I am so sorry," she whispered.

His arms tightened around her in a brief, reassuring embrace. "It's not fear that keeps me here, Gillian. It's disappointment."

Suddenly everything was clear to Gillian. All uncertainty was erased, all doubts dissipated. It was as though her entire life had been preparing her for this moment and she had never been more sure of anything.

"I'm going to help you look for the cure, Gabriel. Maybe we'll never find it, maybe it will be another lifetime wasted, but it will be a lifetime together. Learning from you, working together... and we might succeed. Maybe I'm the key, maybe something I have to offer will be just the thing you need to find the cure."

He smiled, but could not disguise the lingering sadness in his eyes. It puzzled her, and she wanted more than anything to erase it.

"And can it be only a moment ago that you were trying to escape this place, running away from me at peril to your own life?"

She wanted to avert her eyes in shame, but bravely held his gaze. "I didn't know you then, and what I didn't know frightened me. All I ever wanted was the truth. That was all it took to make me free to love you."

It was he who lowered his eyes, rich dark lashes shadowing his cheekbones. "Gillian," he said huskily, "you are my springtime. My only joy. You make miracles seem possible. But I have to tell you..." And he raised his eyes to her. "This grand passion we share will soon fade. You will grown tired of me and chafe against the confines of this place. You'll want children, your quiet home, your tree-lined streets. I can offer you none of those."

Gillian touched his cheek gently, adoring the feel of his skin, soft and rough, smooth and strong. "I'll miss it," she answered honestly. "But I can live without those things. Having known you, I can't live without you now. I could never grow tired of you. It would take me ten lifetimes just to discover all the things I'm going to love about you. My only regret is that there isn't enough time to love you the way I want to... forever."

His arms came around her in a crushing embrace; she felt the deep inhalation of his breath against her neck. And just when the strength of his arms was almost painful, he released her slowly and looked soberly into her eyes. "Gillian," he said, "there is something I want to show you."

THE SIGHT OF the high-tech piece of equipment in such antique surroundings gave Gillian an odd little chill, although she couldn't say why that should be so. But from the time they entered Gabriel's private quarters, the uneasiness that had gripped her on waking seized her again, as though it was all a dream and she was about to awake and lose it all.

He moved his hand beneath the ledge of an oversize desk and a motorized monitor revealed itself. It looked like a computer screen, but when Gillian drew closer she saw it was much more.

The images on the screen were crisp and in color, and if they had not been enhanced by digital markings and trajectory maps like those seen on airplanes and infrared scopes, Gillian would have been tempted to believe what she was seeing was a television show. But the truth was all too clear. Somehow, some part of her had expected it all along.

Two helicopters circled overhead. In the rugged mountain desert below, what appeared to be a squadron of searchers fanned out with radios and rescue packs. There were native guides. There were jeeps. There were burrows and mules. Watching the circus, Gillian felt a sickness form in the pit of her stomach. She groped for the chair behind her and sat down.

"My God!"

"They have heat-sensing devices," Gabriel remarked absently. "Interesting."

Gillian raised eyes to him that were heavy with dread. "How far away are they?"

Gabriel made a few motions near the screen. The full sleeve of his robe brushed her shoulder, his clean warm scent wafted over her. She ached with longing, with needing, with missing him already.

"Five-point-eight kilometers," he replied. "The helicopters, if they continue their present search pattern, should be directly overhead in less than three hours."

"My God," she repeated dully. The coldness that had started in her stomach had spread to her throat, and she lifted her hand there, as though she could massage the emptiness away. "My father—I should have known. I did know—I told you he wouldn't let me just disappear, he wouldn't give up, he would come for me, I knew it. Oh God, Gabriel, what are we going to do?"

His face was utterly unreadable. "What do you want to do?" he asked.

She stared at him, barely comprehending the question. "I want them to go away!" she cried at last. "I want you to be safe, I don't want them to find you—"

"I am safe, Gillian. I have kept this place safe for centuries and they won't find me now unless I want them to."

Gillian thrust both hands into her hair, shaking her head adamantly. "You don't understand! They have satellite photos now, infrared sensors. No one has ever *looked* for you before, Gabriel, and you don't know my father. He'll put the entire force of the U.S. Army behind this search if he has to. He won't give up!"

"They won't find me," Gabriel repeated calmly. His eyes were probing and strong, yet cautious. "They've come for you, Gillian," he said simply. "Will you go?"

Again she merely stared at him, hardly believing what she had heard, much less forming an answer. Then her eyes were drawn almost against her will back to the screen. The beating blades of the helicopters. The young men and women in desert camouflage. The Mylar tents, the painted jeeps... civilization. Home. She tried to conjure up a yearning for it, but she couldn't.

Then she thought of her mother weeping in her bed at night, of her father pacing the floor, of her colleagues who doubtless blamed themselves for her disappearance. She would have been less than human if she had not felt something for their grief. And, yes, she was torn. For that brief moment she was torn.

Gabriel must have seen something in her eyes, for she felt a change come over him. He stood a little straighter, turning from the screen. "There may not be another chance for you to leave this place safely, Gillian," he said. "I won't keep you if you want to go."

It was a moment before she could get her breath and form the words. "No!" She reached for him, but he was standing too far away. She pushed up from the chair. "No, I don't want to go, I told you that! I want to stay here with you."

There was a quick flare of hope in his eyes, which was just as quickly subdued. His struggle to keep his expression neutral broke her heart. "This is a big decision," he said, turning away. "It should not be made in haste. I'll leave you to consider it. The news of the outsiders has spread quickly and some of the people are alarmed. I must do what I can to calm them."

And without looking back, he left the room.

# Chapter Thirteen

Gillian stared at the images on the screen, drawn to them, fascinated by them as though they wove some dread spell of their own. They were looking for her. They were coming for her. They cared about her, they worried about her... yet those people, those machines, those remnants of the world she had left behind, seemed as alien to her as a newsreel about a faraway place and people she had never met. And inside her head a little voice was chanting over and over again, *Go away, go away, please go away...*

She pressed her fingers to her temples, hard, trying to blot out the voices and the images that marched through her mind even after she had turned her back on the screen. God, how could everything have turned so upside down in such a short time? Only a short while ago she had been running from Gabriel, and now she would give all she had ever known or hoped to be just to stay with him, safe from the horrors on that monitor, for a little while longer. Moments ago she had found heaven in Gabriel's arms, and there she had thought she would stay forever, and now it was all being torn from her. She had thought she'd faced the biggest crisis of her life there on the ledge, but that was nothing. That was only the beginning.

The real horror was outside and closing in fast. The real terror was pounding inside her chest as she tried desperately to find some way to keep Gabriel safe without losing him.

She left the room, moving through the honeycomb of chambers until she came to the one where she had confronted him with such petty vitriol only— Could it be true? Had it been only two days ago? At the doorway to the small room she stopped, arrested by the painting that was displayed on the easel. It was finished, and she was stunned to find herself gazing at her own features.

She stepped inside, moving up to the easel. She lifted a hand and lightly touched the edge of the canvas. Her eyes filled unexpectedly with tears. "Oh, Gabriel," she whispered.

A voice spoke behind her, quietly. "They are coming closer."

It was Phillipe. Gillian swallowed hard and turned, blotting ineffectually at her damp cheeks. "I know."

Phillipe's visage seemed to have aged in the short time she had known him. She recognized that too was her fault. "It will break his heart if you leave," he said soberly.

"I know."

She wondered which was worse: to die of the pain losing him would cause her, or to live with it... forever.

She swallowed again, took a steadying breath and squared her shoulders. "It's my fault they've come," she said. "I can't let them find this place. I can't let them find *him.*"

Her voice almost broke, but she fought fiercely for control. She lifted her chin another inch; with all the will at her command she kept her voice steady. "Gabriel said there was a map that would show me how to get out of here."

The emotions that crossed Phillipe's face were clear to read, his struggle evident. But he had spent too many years protecting Gabriel, and in the end there was only one decision he could make. Just as, for Gillian, there had been only one possible decision from the beginning.

"It's in the library," he said, and he turned to lead the way.

GABRIEL'S PEACEFUL sanctuary had been invaded by chaos, and the invaders were still miles away. Most of the time he lived here in sublime indifference to those who occupied the space he had built. Their lives had nothing to do with him, and he was dimly surprised now at how much this society seemed to have been built around his presence here over the centuries.

Mechanisms to guard against intruders or escape had fallen into place the moment the presence of outsiders was discovered, and Gabriel supposed he must have designed those plans himself when he—and the world—were young and defence against aggression was second nature for all of humankind.

Functions and drills that had heretofore been merely ceremonial were now brought into practice, and Gabriel made no effort to stop them—he was not, in fact, even sure he could. With the same logic they employed to welcome an injured stranger into their midst, these people would defend themselves against what they perceived as an attack from outsiders, and it was their right to do so.

Gabriel knew, however, that no heroics would be required and the threat existed mostly in the minds of those who were determined to fight it. No one outside these walls would ever find that place. He had seen to that long ago.

The only threat the images on the screen posed for him lay within the memories they brought back for Gillian, memories of all *they* could offer her that *he* could not. The only fear he had of them was that they would take her away from him, and if he could have stopped them with weapons of technology or his bare hands, he would have done so. But Gillian's will was the one thing that had never been within his power to control. If it had been, he would not have loved her half as much.

He stood at the console, gazing at the busy searchers with their radios and vehicles and their maps neatly divided into quadrants, and he heard Phillipe's footsteps behind him. He pulled out a panel beneath the desk, touched another series of buttons and replaced the panel again before acknowledging his presence. He did not have to turn around to know the news Phillipe had brought. He tried to steel himself against it.

"She is gone?" Gabriel said.

Phillipe answered quietly, "Yes."

He thought he was prepared, but the news struck Gabriel like a blow between the shoulder blades; he actually stiffened against it. He had been so sure... Yet what choice did she have? A life of isolation and deprivation here with him or the rich, full life of contributions and challenges she had left behind. Still, he had been so sure...of her, of them, of the glory they had found in each other.

"Odd," he said when he could speak. His voice was hoarse. "I know it can't be true, but as I look back it seems to me now that she was the only woman I've ever truly loved. In a hundred lifetimes...the only one."

Phillipe took a step closer. Out of the corner of his eye he saw the other man lift a hand as though to touch his shoulder, then let it drop. Gabriel should have been moved by his friend's concern, but he was not. His own pain was too great.

"There are things in life we can't prevent," Phillipe said. "You know that. She was an extraordinary woman and I'm sorry it had to end this way. If it comforts you to know it, her motives were not selfish. She was afraid they would find you with all of their advanced sensors and special equipment. She knew they wouldn't give up as long as she was still missing. So she went to them—to save you."

Gabriel turned around slowly, his face taut with shock. "Do you mean—it wasn't her choice? She went to save me?"

Phillipe nodded.

"But there was no need!" Gabriel cried. "I told her there was no need! I just activated a protective screen the most advanced army in the world will not be able to penetrate for a hundred years! Blast her and her stubborn impetuosity—I told her I could protect this place!" And suddenly he was seized with urgency. He caught Phillipe's arm, hard. "Who is guiding her out?" he demanded.

All the color drained from Phillipe's face. His lips barely moved as he whispered, "No one. I...gave her a map."

It seemed it took forever for the words to register. Even when he comprehended their significance, it seemed another lifetime passed before he could make his body respond. All he could do was stare at Phillipe and say hoarsely, "You didn't let her go alone. The Protectors are under orders of war. They'll kill her if she tries to leave this place!"

Phillipe's face crumpled, and he said brokenly, "I didn't mean—I'm so sorry. I only wanted to—"

But Gabriel had flung him away and was already running for the door. "Get my healing bag!"

Heart pounding, limbs stretching, Gabriel ran. And he knew—he must have known, deep inside him—it was already too late.

GABRIEL HAD SEEN a thousand men fall in battle. He had seen disease and accident and violence snatch away countless human lives and he had been touched by each one in his own way. But until that moment, until he saw Gillian fall, he had never felt the pierce of death's arrow through his own soul, he had never understood what it meant.

He reached the first exit tunnel and found the emergency lighting there already activated by the passage of another person. He hoped it was only a guard, but when he rounded the corner he saw Gillian, less than a hundred feet ahead of him. He shouted her name.

"Gillian!"

The syllables echoed throughout the tunnel. She turned. Her dark hair whirled about her, separate strands lifted in the wind, he saw the surprise on her face, the way she half lifted her hand toward him, as though in supplication, or goodbye. And when he thought back later, he wondered, over and over again, whether it all might have been different if she hadn't turned at the moment, if he hadn't called out....

For it all happened in an instant. Before he'd called her name, the killing blow had been launched. As she turned, the razor-sharp blade was hurtling through the air. Instinctively he must have known it, because he found himself suddenly rooted to the spot, unable to run any longer, one hand raised to her but too far away to reach her. And just as her hand started to lift toward him, the blade found its target.

Gillian crumpled to the ground, pierced through the heart by a dagger.

Gabriel screamed, *"Noooo..."* And the cry seemed to reverberate forever, through the subterranean corridors of this mountain paradise and down the corridors of time, a single endless syllable that wound around and twisted in on itself and seemed to encompass all the anguish of all mankind's history. *"Noooo..."*

He ran toward her, lurching, stumbling, falling. His legs were too slow, and the air was like syrup, pushing him back, keeping him away from her. He dropped to his knees beside her, pulling the blade from her body, scooping her up into his arms. In that instant he forgot all his skill, all his knowledge, and he sank back into an instinct as old as time. He pressed her close, holding her tight, rocking her back and forth as though his strength, his love and his will alone could infuse life back into her. And he did not know how long he remained like that, holding her, wasting precious moments.

But when Phillipe sank down beside him and laid a comforting hand on his shoulder, Gabriel jerked away violently. He was galvanized into action, gently laying Gillian down again in a pool of her own blood, snatching the bag from Phillipe, spilling the contents on the ground.

He made a crude compress to stop the bleeding. He checked her pulse and found none. He injected her with stimulants, healing accelerators, cardio-regulators. He checked her pulse again. He listened for a breath.

"Malik," Phillipe ventured hesitantly, sadly, "she has lost too much blood...."

"I'm not going to lose her," Gabriel growled fiercely. "I saved her before, I can do it again."

"This time is different. She is gone, Malik. She doesn't breathe, her heart has no blood to pump. Let her go."

Furiously Gabriel flung Phillipe away as he tried to offer a comforting touch. Desperately he began performing artificial respiration on Gillian.

He did not know how long he kept it up. There was no response. The bleeding had stopped, but her heart refused to beat, her lungs refused to breathe. That essential spark that was Gillian was fading, fading, and he could taste death on her lips. His face was damp, though whether with tears or perspiration he did now know, and he thought desperately, *If I could trade places with you for one moment ... if I could give you my genes even at the expense of my own life, I would.*

Suddenly he sat up and, snatching a scalpel from the bag, he ripped open the sleeve of his robe. Phillipe cried in alarm, "What are you doing?"

"Prepare a transfusion tube," Gabriel barked. "Now!"

"But you—you can't! You don't know what it will do to her. You've never given anyone else your blood before."

"I know it might save her life!" Gabriel snapped back. "That's all I need to know. Do as I say!"

And, as Phillipe fumbled in the bag for the necessary equipment, Gabriel made a quick, sharp cut in the prominent vein of his inner arm. He could not wait for the proper transfusion equipment. Quickly, before he began to heal, he made a similar incision in Gillian's arms and placed his wound against hers. "Forgive me, my love," he whispered, leaning close to her, "if I should bring this curse upon you. Only, come back to me...."

Their blood mingled.

Gabriel closed his eyes tightly and prayed. He felt Phillipe grown very still beside him. And then he felt—he thought he felt—a soft inhalation of breath.

He looked down at her just as Gillian's eyes fluttered open. The wonder that flowed through him was as sweet as sunshine. For a moment he couldn't speak, he couldn't move.

Gillian's eyes, focusing on him, lost the dazed, frightened look that accompanies illness and became filled with peace.

"Gabriel," she murmured. "Are we safe?"

"Beloved." Gently, hardly daring to touch her for fear he might discover she was only an illusion, he brushed her forehead with his fingertips. "We are safe."

She sighed and turned her face to his touch, closing her eyes in a natural sleep. Gabriel bent and kissed her forehead. Then he straightened, staring at the bloody smear his touch had left on her skin.

He looked at his arm. He looked at Phillipe, whose face reflected the same stunned shock Gabriel's did. The eyes of both men returned to the wound Gabriel had made in his arm.

It had not healed. It was still bleeding.

# Chapter Fourteen

Gillian awoke in a softly lit room with the memory of gentle dreams floating around her like clouds. She was warm, she was comfortable, she was surrounded by softness—the soft yellow gauze of a bed that was canopied with a profusion of romantic netting drawn back in places with gilded medallions, festooned and draped overhead so that the impression was indeed like floating on a cloud. The massive four-poster bed that was adorned by gilded cherubs and climbing vines.

*Just like a fairy-tale palace,* she thought drowsily. *Home. I'm home.*

She turned her head and saw Gabriel sitting in the chair beside her bed, and she knew it was true. She *was* home.

She stretched out her arm for him and he was beside her, gathering her into his embrace. They shared one fierce, breathless moment too intense for words, and then Gillian smoothed back his hair with a shaking hand. She pushed a little away, looking at him. "You saved my life," she whispered. "Again."

He smiled. "You were too valuable to lose."

"There's a lot I don't remember, I don't understand—"

"And none of it is important." He raised a finger as though to quiet her. "I'll explain it all later."

She searched his face anxiously. "You said we were safe. I remember you saying that. Have they gone away?"

Gabriel's lashes dropped slowly; tenderly, he placed a kiss atop her head. "Yes, beloved. They're gone."

"Because I want you to know—Gabriel, I didn't want to leave, but it was the only way I could think of to keep them away from you."

"Then you're not sorry?" he said seriously. "You're not sorry they've gone and left you behind?"

In response, she wrapped her arms around his neck and held him tightly. "No," she whispered. "All I ever wanted is right here . . . in my arms."

He caught her face and kissed her hard, leaving Gillian breathless and tingling for more. "I'm glad, Gillian," he whispered. "I'm so glad."

When he released her, Gillian's head was spinning, but still she caught a glimpse of something unsettling when his sleeve fell away as he lifted his arm. It was a square gauze bandage.

Her first instinct was womanly concern. It was only a second later that the real meaning of the bandage on the inside of his arm began to sink in, and she stared at it, dry-mouthed and unable to speak for a long time.

"Gabriel," she managed at last. "What happened?"

His expression was very sober, his eyes penetrating, asking questions and finding the answers without words. "I've run the tests, and the viral component in my blood is gone. It appears that when I was trying to save your life with my blood, you passed an essential antibody to me instead. I've also tested your blood," he added quickly, "and there's no indication that you've been contaminated by the defect I suffered with so long. Gillian," he said quietly, and both his hands closed over hers, "you have cured me. I'm a normal man, with a normal span of life to live. You have given me . . . the only gift I have ever wished for."

Gillian's fingers went to her lips, as though to still her runaway breath or perhaps a cry. In truth, she couldn't make a sound. She could hardly comprehend any of it, nor begin to absorb its significance. In the end all she could say was "But, Gabriel, I— What will happen to you? How can you act as though this is a good thing? I never meant to—I never wanted—"

As she broke off in helpless confusion, his expression softened. "What will happen to me is that I will begin to age and die—just as you will, just as will hundreds upon thousands upon millions of people around the world. And it is a good thing, my love. The best thing. You've given me a chance to live the only life I've ever wanted. With you."

Gillian drew in a slow, deep breath, too filled with wonder and joy to give way to words. She embraced him fiercely, tightly, for a long moment. Then he looked down at her, his eyes shining with possibilities she had never seen before, with hope, with joy...with youth.

"Gillian, there is no need to stay here if you want. We can leave this place whenever you want and go wherever you want. I can show you the world."

"Someday," Gillian murmured, suffused by a joy greater than any she had ever known. She drew him down beside her. "Someday maybe we will. After all, the future is ours."

And so it was.

Meet four of the most mysterious, magical men...in

These men are more than tall, dark and handsome. They have extraordinary powers that make them "more than men." But whether they are able to grant you three wishes or live forever, make no mistake—their greatest, most extraordinary power is that of seduction.

This March, make a date with the last MORE THAN MEN:

#525   CINDERMAN by Anne Stuart

## THE BABY IS ADORABLE...
## BUT WHICH MAN IS HIS DADDY?

*Alec Roman:* He found baby Andy in a heart-shaped Valentine basket—
but were finders necessarily keepers?

*Jack Rourke:* During his personal research into Amish culture, he got close
to an Amish beauty—so close he thought he was the father.

*Grady Noland:* The tiny bundle of joy softened this rogue cop—and
made him want to own up to what he thought were
his responsibilities.

Cathy Gillen Thacker brings you TOO MANY DADS, a three-book series that
asks the all-important question: Which man is about to become a daddy?

*Meet the potential fathers in:*
**#521 BABY ON THE DOORSTEP**
 **February 1994**
**#526 DADDY TO THE RESCUE**
 **March 1994**
**#529 TOO MANY MOMS**
 **April 1994**

DADS

# *My Valentine*
## 1994

Celebrate the most romantic day of the year with
*MY VALENTINE 1994*
a collection of original stories, written by
four of Harlequin's most popular authors...

**MARGOT DALTON**
**MURIEL JENSEN**
**MARISA CARROLL**
**KAREN YOUNG**

Available in February, wherever
Harlequin Books are sold.

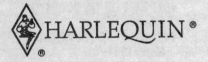

# HARLEQUIN ®
®

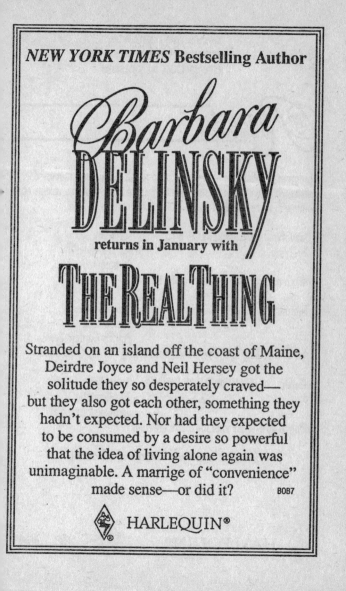

**Relive the romance...
Harlequin and Silhouette
are proud to present**

*by* Request ™

A program of collections of three complete novels by the most requested
authors with the most requested themes. Be sure to look for one volume each
month with three complete novels by top name authors.

In January:    **WESTERN LOVING**    Susan Fox
                                      JoAnn Ross
                                      Barbara Kaye

*Loving a cowboy is easy—taming him isn't!*

In February:   **LOVER, COME BACK!**   Diana Palmer
                                       Lisa Jackson
                                       Patricia Gardner Evans

*It was over so long ago—yet now they're calling, "Lover, Come Back!"*

In March:      **TEMPERATURE RISING**   JoAnn Ross
                                        Tess Gerritsen
                                        Jacqueline Diamond

*Falling in love—just what the doctor ordered!*

**Available at your favorite retail outlet.**

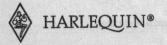

**HARLEQUIN®**

Don't miss these Harlequin favorites by some of our most distinguished authors!
And now, you can receive a discount by ordering two or more titles!

| | | | |
|---|---|---|---|
| HT#25409 | THE NIGHT IN SHINING ARMOR by JoAnn Ross | $2.99 | ☐ |
| HT#25471 | LOVESTORM by JoAnn Ross | $2.99 | ☐ |
| HP#11463 | THE WEDDING by Emma Darcy | $2.89 | ☐ |
| HP#11592 | THE LAST GRAND PASSION by Emma Darcy | $2.99 | ☐ |
| HR#03188 | DOUBLY DELICIOUS by Emma Goldrick | $2.89 | ☐ |
| HR#03248 | SAFE IN MY HEART by Leigh Michaels | $2.89 | ☐ |
| HS#70464 | CHILDREN OF THE HEART by Sally Garrett | $3.25 | ☐ |
| HS#70524 | STRING OF MIRACLES by Sally Garrett | $3.39 | ☐ |
| HS#70500 | THE SILENCE OF MIDNIGHT by Karen Young | $3.39 | ☐ |
| HI#22178 | SCHOOL FOR SPIES by Vickie York | $2.79 | ☐ |
| HI#22212 | DANGEROUS VINTAGE by Laura Pender | $2.89 | ☐ |
| HI#22219 | TORCH JOB by Patricia Rosemoor | $2.89 | ☐ |
| HAR#16459 | MACKENZIE'S BABY by Anne McAllister | $3.39 | ☐ |
| HAR#16466 | A COWBOY FOR CHRISTMAS by Anne McAllister | $3.39 | ☐ |
| HAR#16462 | THE PIRATE AND HIS LADY by Margaret St. George | $3.39 | ☐ |
| HAR#16477 | THE LAST REAL MAN by Rebecca Flanders | $3.39 | ☐ |
| HH#28704 | A CORNER OF HEAVEN by Theresa Michaels | $3.99 | ☐ |
| HH#28707 | LIGHT ON THE MOUNTAIN by Maura Seger | $3.99 | ☐ |

### *Harlequin Promotional Titles*

| | | | |
|---|---|---|---|
| #83247 | YESTERDAY COMES TOMORROW by Rebecca Flanders | $4.99 | ☐ |
| #83257 | MY VALENTINE 1993 | $4.99 | ☐ |
| | (short-story collection featuring Anne Stuart, Judith Arnold, Anne McAllister, Linda Randall Wisdom) | | |

**(limited quantities available on certain titles)**

| | | | |
|---|---|---|---|
| | **AMOUNT** | $ | |
| **DEDUCT:** | **10% DISCOUNT FOR 2+ BOOKS** | $ | |
| **ADD:** | **POSTAGE & HANDLING** | $ | |
| | ($1.00 for one book, 50¢ for each additional) | | |
| | **APPLICABLE TAXES*** | $ _____ | |
| | **TOTAL PAYABLE** | $ _____ | |
| | (check or money order—please do not send cash) | | |

To order, complete this form and send it, along with a check or money order for the total above, payable to Harlequin Books, to: **In the U.S.:** 3010 Walden Avenue, P.O. Box 9047, Buffalo, NY 14269-9047; **In Canada:** P.O. Box 613, Fort Erie, Ontario, L2A 5X3.

Name: _____

Address: _____ City: _____

State/Prov.: _____ Zip/Postal Code: _____

*New York residents remit applicable sales taxes.
 Canadian residents remit applicable GST and provincial taxes.

HBACK-JM